Short Stories and Tall Tales

Book II

by
E.P. Whitney, PhD

Bloomington, IN   Milton Keynes, UK

AuthorHouse™
1663 Liberty Drive, Suite 200
Bloomington, IN 47403
www.authorhouse.com
Phone: 1-800-839-8640

AuthorHouse™ UK Ltd.
500 Avebury Boulevard
Central Milton Keynes, MK9 2BE
www.authorhouse.co.uk
Phone: 08001974150

This book is a work of fiction. People, places, events, and situations are the product of the author's imagination. Any resemblance to actual persons, living or dead, or historical events, is purely coincidental.

© 2006 E.P. Whitney, PhD. All rights reserved.

No part of this book may be reproduced, stored in a retrieval system, or transmitted by any means without the written permission of the author.

First published by AuthorHouse 2/22/2006

ISBN: 1-4208-8888-9 (sc)

Printed in the United States of America
Bloomington, Indiana

This book is printed on acid-free paper.

CONTENTS

BEYOND GENDER   1

Thomas O'Finnigan McDonough was a banker, then a priest who redefined freedom and sex for his diversified community. Does man have the right to take away the freedom given to us by God.?

THE RELUCTANT WITNESS   45

The story of War and Peace in the South Pacific and an en-counter with God as seen through the eyes of a young teen-age sailor. Innocent Eric Jones is forced to hate, then to love, and finally to make peace with his maker

THE JEWISH YANKEE   75

Part I - An unbelievable story, never before told, of an American Jew trapped in Nazi Germany!

Part II - The Jewish Yankee finds the "Promised Land."

THE VOLUPTUOUS CORPS   95

A murder mystery solved by the parish priest.

A CATASTROPHIC OBSESSION   103

For God and Country - Or What?

FOREWORD

Beyond gender, beyond race, and beyond ethnicity lies the human being. When we come to the realization that there are as many profound differences between women and women, men and men, black and black, white and white, and within each ethnic group as there is between women and men, black and white, and one ethnic group and another; we will begin to understand the true identity of a human being. Society has established categories and restrictions in a culture that equates humanity to a mathematical equation. Scientific reasoning, the measure for materialism, groups matter into strict categories. H_2O is water, CO_2 is carbon dioxide, etc. Society has also grouped human beings into like divisions: gender, race, ethnicity; and a number of other fine lines of distinction. The problem lies in the fact that human beings are more than material entities; and division by material characteristics gives a completely distorted description of the individual human .Society has also labeled and categorized the human into functional and social classifications which further distorts the true identity of the individual. We are at the point where we have become a horde of individuals who are completely unaware of the identity of other individuals as well as our own identity. Many philosophers of our time have suggested that we look beyond our societal and cultural heritage and examine ourselves as the humans we were intended to be; not the categorizations that man has adapted to his materialistic world.

BEYOND GENDER

Introduction

Thomas O'Finnigan McDonough's mother was an alcoholic and his father was an addicted gambler; but in spite of these apparently disabling afflictions, his parents provided him with a loving, caring childhood. Thomas's mother, Molly McDonough drank herself into a happy state of inebriation every night of the week, but never once did she neglect her duties to her family from breakfast to the preparation of the dinner meal in the evening. Thomas P. McDonough, better know as "Junior," frittered away a family fortune over the years, but he always managed to provide food for the table and a roof overhead.The grandparents of Thomas O'Finnigan McDonough, Shawn O'Finnigan and Thomas P. McDonough, Sr., better known as "Teepe," were the role models that influenced his life. Shawn came to America from the streets of Dublin as an 18 year old lad and worked his way up the ladder as a construction worker. "Teepe was born in Bellfast, but he was settled in an elegant house on "Nob Hill" with his parents and grandparents before he learned to walk. With a name like Thomas O'Finnigan McDonough and an unusual heritage like his, one would expect a rather unusual future for this young man, and indeed it was. This story has to be told as fiction. If you find any of the characters that you can identify as known persons, living or dead, please consider it a coincidence.

Chapter I - A Change Of Objective

This story of Thomas O'Finnigan McDonough starts shortly after his 52nd birthday. Thomas went to work at the bank for his grandfather "Teepe" right after college, and he kept his nose to the grindstone six days a week. Sundays however were spent with granddad, Shawn O'Finnigan. Both of Thomas's grandmothers had passed on when he was very young, and most of his life had been spent with a strong male influence.

Thomas was devastated when Molly and Junior were consumed by fire at night in their home while he was still in college. That night was a special night for the parents of Thomas O'Finnigan McDonough. Molly was in her usually festive mood and Junior had joined her. Their bodies were found in the bedroom and the coroner said that they never woke up.

Grand dad Shawn, dedicated every Sunday as "Thomas' Birthday," and he made every one a special treat for his grandson. Shawn was not much of a businessman, but he provided the support Thomas needed when Teepe died suddenly with a heart attack and left the controlling interest in the Bank to his only living relative, Thomas. Thomas was only 40 years old at the time, and running the bank was an enormous challenge for him. But, bolstered by his Sunday excursions, and Shawn's encouragement, Thomas was very successful.

At age 51, the light of his life, Grand dad Shawn, left this earth to meet his maker. Old Shawn was a devoted Catholic, and he was a great influence on Thomas's religious convictions, but he never once tried to dissuade Thomas from the "Church of England" as he used to call it. With Shawn gone, the Bank and life in general, seemed to have little meaning for Thomas. He sold his interest in the business and put his money into government bonds.

Thomas decided to spend the rest of his life as a "Servant of God," and enrolled in a nondenominational theological college. Thanks to the influence of a generous donation, he was ordained in one year, and now he was looking for a church in which to serve.

Thomas had several churches to investigate and decided to look at St. Thomas, located in the suburbs with a 'mixed' socioeconomic congregation. Of course, St. Thomas wanted to look him over as well.

Thomas didn't look much like a fat prosperous banker. He was tall and thin with wavy black hair and a pair of kind blue eyes that looked like they just couldn't say no to anything. But Thomas could say no in a very direct way. He was a very serious person and spoke as if every work was money and he didn't want to waste a cent. When Thomas said something, people who knew him listened, because they knew that what he had to say was important or he wouldn't say it.

Chapter II - A Call to St. Thomas Church

When Thomas was interviewed by the St. Thomas Vestry, he was confronted by all kinds of questions. One question, asked by the newest and youngest member of the Vestry concerned him the most.

"Would you support a monthly 'Casino Night' at the Parish House? I think it would be a great money maker," squeaked the shallow neophyte.

St. Thomas Church had been founded by an ultra conservative group who were well known for their opposition to gambling of any kind. In fact, it was the notoriety of the former Pastor's outburst against Bingo that caught his attention in the first place. In view of his father's former affliction, Thomas had thought that this might be a message from on high that this was the church he was destined to serve. A Casino Night? Even the most liberal Churches don't have a Casino Night, thought Thomas.

"What do you believe in?" asked Thomas. The entire Vestry stared at him as if they could not believe what Thomas had said.

"Just what do you believe in?" Thomas repeated.

The eldest of the vestrymen cleared his throat and answered in a somewhat hesitant voice, "We believe in God, and - and his Son Jesus Christ!"

"And the Holy Spirit too, I'm sure," countered Thomas; "But I mean beyond that, and in support of this proposal!"

"We believe in Freedom," blurted out the young vestryman who had posed the Casino question.

"Freedom," grumbled another vestryman, "Freedom is what has gotten us into the mess we are in."

As if this was a signal to start a brawl, the rest of the Vestry started spouting off about freedom, all talking at once with increasingly loud voices making it impossible to discern any understandable statement made by anyone. Thomas felt that it was about time for him to take over, and that is just what he did.

"I understand that you would like to have me preach this Sunday, and possibly one or two more Sundays. Let me ask you a few questions to give me an idea as to what would be best for me to speak about.

It was as if Thomas was speaking in a foreign language. His statements quieted the room, but it was obvious that no one had even started to think about what was to said be in his sermons. This group was interested in the financial affairs of the Church. As far as they were concerned, business was their job and business was the most important topic that there was to discuss. Of course, if anything was said to offend or make them uncomfortable, that would be a different story to be sure.

Thomas continued, "It sounds like Freedom is a very important part of your philosophy, and yet I heard an expression against freedom. Could we talk a little bit about this?"

The young vestryman who declared freedom as a major part of their faith spoke first. "Many churches are like this church used to be; they only want their own kind of people to join and attend. In America we don't believe in discriminating against people because they are a little different than we are. It is a free society where anyone can go where they want to go, do what they want to do, and join whatever they want to join."

The vestryman who had grumbled against freedom countered with, "We should also have the freedom to associate with the people who are compatible with us and those we want to associate with. If everyone has the freedom to do whatever they want to, it takes away the freedom of everyone else!"

It seemed like there was a stalemate and something like, "Your freedom ends where the other person's freedom begins," would just not solve this conflict.

"It's getting late," said Thomas, "And I should get busy preparing my sermon for next Sunday. Perhaps I can come up with some food for thought in my sermon and we can discuss this further at our next meeting." With that the meeting was adjourned.

Thomas spent the remainder of the week in the Rectory. It was a big, beautiful old building, but so lonely. The regular house- keeper left when the last Rector retired and an interim housekeeper had been hired, but she only came in the morning and left after cleaning up the evening dishes. Thomas was used to being alone, but he lived in a fairly modest home with only enough furniture to meet his needs. This Rectory was a mansion. The front hall and foyer were nearly as large as his former living room; and there were art works and expensive looking pictures everywhere. There were eight bedrooms upstairs and eight separate bathrooms, one adjoining each bedroom.

"What an absolute waste," Thomas thought to himself. Thomas always had more money than he could spend after "Teepe" died and left him his

Short Stories and Tall Tales 9

interest in the Bank, but he was never extravagant. Waste was a sin as far as he was concerned and he couldn't help thinking what he would do with the property if he were selected as the parish priest.

"Enough day dreaming," Thomas said to himself as he shook his head to come back to reality. He had a sermon to prepare, and it might be a sermon that determined whether he would be the priest at this church or not. The rest of the time was spent writing and rewriting with only breaks for meals or a snack.

CHAPTER III - FREEDOM

When the congregation saw the title of the Reverend Thomas O'Finnigan McDonough's sermon posted on the church sign, several suggested that they contact the CIA! - "Freedom Has Become The Curse of America!"

In spite of the opposition to the title of the sermon, the church was packed on Sunday morning; and when Thomas delivered his thesis, he had the complete attention of everyone in the church.

"Freedom has become the most abused, confused and misused concept in America today," Thomas started with his most stern and authoritative voice.

"As Americans, most of us feel that freedom means the right to do what we want to do whenever we want to do it. Most even feel that being a Christian means to be free to worship God as you wish. My friends, being a Christian means to give up your freedom; freely. Being a Christian means putting the welfare of everyone else above your own. Being a Christian means to be a complete slave to the will of God! Freedom is a divine gift from God. It was meant to be shared and it was meant to be given to others. 'As freely as ye have received, so shall you give.' 'It is more blessed to give than to receive!' Does anyone recall where these quotes were taken from, and who said them?

Of course you know that these were the words of our Lord, and they can be found in the Gospels! Somewhere in the evolving of Western Society, we have taken the selfish approach to freedom. Freedom has become the license to exploit others and the right to satisfy our own desires regardless of the consequences to others. We have used freedom to become greedy and corrupt. Many Government officials have betrayed their trust and used their offices for their own personal gain. Many Business Leaders have cheated and stolen their way to enormous fortunes. But, before we become too outraged and self-righteous, let me add that many church leaders have betrayed an even greater trust. Yes, Freedom has become our curse! It has become the means to rationalize our greed and selfishness as a God given right. It has allowed us to abandon the teachings of Jesus and become the 'people of the lie.'

Were I to become your Pastor, I would pray and work to overcome this curse and turn this church into a body for giving to others. Church suppers would become free meals for the poor and hungry. The Ladies' Rummage Sale would clothe the needy and forget about their contribution to the church budget."

It was hard to determine how the congregation had taken the rash statements made in the sermon. As one might expect in judging from Thomas's secure financial condition, he was not the least bit concerned about not getting a job, but he really thought that he could make a difference in this church and he found himself anxious to find out what the people thought about him.

Chapter IV - A New Beginning

For some undetermined reason, Thomas was offered the position at St. Thomas. You would think that he was coming into a church where most of the congregation thought as he did and were eager and willing to support his thesis of giving and sharing with others. However, this was not exactly the case.

Most of the people were concerned for others and were willing to share, as long as it did not interfere with their own welfare and comfort. This sounds perfectly reasonable for a society steeped in 'Individualism' and the 'Protestant Work Ethic." The rub comes in the fact that most of the people were still struggling to reach their 'comfort plain,' and they strongly felt that it was their God Given right and duty to rise up to the highest comfort plain possible. Unfortunately, as human nature has it, no matter how much we have, it never seems to be quite enough.

In spite of mass apathetic resistance, the Parish managed to put on two dinners for the needy, one at Thanksgiving and one at Christmas. They also operated a Thrift Shop one day a week and kept a 'free section' generously supplied with clothing. Thomas would have liked to do more, but his attention was drawn to the welfare of his own congregation.

Over half of the families in the church had come from broken homes, and although most had regrouped with second marriages and joint custody arrangements, there was constant friction between over-protective and irresponsible spouses as well as step parent squabbles and sibling rivalries. Thomas was called upon to give counseling in an area in which he had no experience and little formal training. In desperation, Thomas sought help from the Bishop.

The Bishop was a very large man, six foot six inches tall and nearly 300 pounds. He gave the appearance of being very jolly and easy going, but those who knew him well, knew that he was a very practical minded man and that he wanted things done right. "Done right' was interpreted as doing as the Bishop wanted it done.

The Bishop took little time in responding to Thomas's call for help. He arrived at 9 o'clock sharp the following Monday morning. It was well past noon however before Thomas had a chance to talk about the counseling of his flock. It seemed that the Bishop was quite concerned about the fact that St. Thomas Church had been tardy in sending in their Diocesan Assessment, and that they were several hundred dollars in arrears at the present time.

Thomas tried to explain that their outreach program in support of the community demanded more than their budget called for, but the Bishop did not appreciate this system of prioritization.

"The main purpose of the Church is the propagation of the Faith!" exclaimed the Bishop who was obviously disturbed that Thomas had not put this as his number one priority. "Over the years," the Bishop continued, "The Church has preserved the presence of God on this sinful earth and has served as a haven for those who chose to follow in the footsteps of our Lord and Savior, Jesus Christ."

There was no doubt about the fact that the Bishop was completely sincere in his belief that the material presence of the Church and the sanctity of ceremony was the saving grace of man kind.

"The poor will always be with us, Thomas. We must fix our attention on things above."

Lunch lasted for an hour and a half! The Bishop had a veracious appetite and Mrs. Murphy, the housekeeper, had to come up with a supplement to her original menu twice during the feast. Finally the senior cleric turned to Thomas and said, "What about this trouble you are having in the Parish?'

It's about family and marriage counseling, your worship. The basic problem, as I see it, is divorce. People are not taking their marriage vows seriously. Perhaps we are too lenient on our stand concerning divorce. Perhaps if we took a hard line, they would think twice before breaking up a family and disrupting young lives."

"Thomas, my boy. Divorce is a vital element of freedom in our society. Take away that freedom, and you take away hope. The laws of our society are based upon the gift of a 'second chance.' We must simply negotiate financial arrangements where all parties can maintain a reasonable standard of living. Life goes on and so must we!"

Continuing the thought, but actually changing the subject, the Bishop went on, "When I was a young Priest, I tried to reconcile two older parishioners who were the backbone of my church. Their commitment to the church was almost half of our budget. The man had been a womanizer all during their marriage and the wife finally put her foot down. We negotiated a settlement that resulted with the man leaving the church and the wife becoming twice the benefactor that they were together!"

"But Bishop," Thomas interrupted, "I'm not talking about finances, I'm concerned about something much bigger than that."

"Thomas! The wife in this case contributed more than just money. The church became her life. She also became the social leader as well, serving on the Alter Guild, the Vestry, the Every Member Canvas and a host of other activities. What you must realize, Thomas, is that we exist in an economic society, and that if we are to survive at all in this society, we must be concerned with economic affairs."

The Bishop was genuinely concerned for Thomas, and in a fatherly gesture, he put his arm around Thomas' shoulder. "You will make out fine, Thomas, just proceed as way opens."

With his parting words of wisdom, the Bishop thanked Thomas for lunch and left the puzzled Priest to solve his own problems.

Less than an hour after the Bishop left the Rectory, there was a knock at the door. Bob Stevens the current treasurer stood there with an intense look of pain on his face. Bob was a rotund man, just over 5 feet tall and close to 250 pounds, but he was always immaculate and neat as a pin. Today however, he was disheveled and looked as if he had spent the night wrestling with a grizzly bear.

" I think I'm going to kill myself," he blurted out.

Thomas just stood there for a moment as if strapped into a straight-jacket. Finally he said, "Come in, come in!" The big hulk fell into a chair, hung his head and stared at the floor.

"Sandy wants a divorce! This was my second chance. When Pat left me, I thought I would die, but along came Sandy and I started over again. It's too much, I just can't go through all of this again."

What does a Pastor do in a case like this? Generally, you preach a sermon to guide the flock along the path of righteousness, urging reform while trying not to offend. But here, we have a crisis. The only salvation is hope! But, false hope can lead to even greater desperation. Perhaps an offer to try to help will give temporary hope that will quiet the patient and give time to come up with an acceptable solution! Thomas decided upon temporary hope.

"Have Sandy come in to see me," Thomas came forth in a forced calm and serene tone. "I'm sure we can work something out." Thomas offered his brooding patient a cup of coffee, and after some small talk, he wished Stevens 'A Good Day,' then settled down to ponder his next move.

Chapter V - Success and More Problems

Later on in the week, Sandy Stevens, Bob's wife, called to make an appointment to speak with her Priest. Sandy was a most attractive brunette with a level head. Her first husband was completely irresponsible, and try as she would, she could not make him settle down. He finally took off with a young girl just out of high school and left Sandy with their four year old daughter. When she met Bob, he seemed to be an answer to her prayers, and they were thought to be an ideal couple.

Sandy arrived for her appointment precisely on time. Thomas O'Finnigan McDonough offered his guest a cup of coffee and kept up a nervous banter of small talk, trying to appear calm and collected; which he was not. Finally, "You know why I'm here, Father," she started. "Bob has become so insecure lately, he's just driving me crazy."

Thomas was most insecure himself, but felt that he saw an opening and interjected. "Bob thinks the world of you, and I know that he would do anything he could to make you happy."

"Then tell him not to fly into a rage every time I ask him to do a little something," she countered in harsh anger. "The other night I asked him to take a picture of my garden. He had taken a picture of my neighbor's garden but didn't bother to take one of mine. He had to go on and on telling me that he had taken many pictures of my garden before, but what did that have to do with it?"

Thomas asked, "Did you tell him that he had taken a picture of his neighbor's garden and should have taken one of yours at that time too?" Sandy cleared her throat, "Well, perhaps I did, and of course, he should have too!"

There was a slight pause, then Thomas added, "Did you have any other illustrations of Bob's outrageous behavior?"

"Yes I do," Sandy snapped. "Just last night I came home tired and with an aching back. I know that he was tired too, and I hated to ask him, but he hadn't rubbed my back in quite a while, so I asked him."

"Did you mention the fact that he hadn't rubbed your back in quite some time?" Thomas questioned.

Sandy thought for a moment, then added, "I did say something about the fact that he seldom rubs my back anymore; and he went on and on about how he gives me a massage whenever I ask for it, and bla, bla, bla," .

"Did he rub your back?" Thomas added.

"Oh yes," Sandy replied, He always does a good job after he gets over all of his arguing. But his jawing just about takes all of the pleasure out of the massage."

Thomas paused a moment, then confronted Sandy. "I think that I can help you without even talking to Bob, if you are willing to listen and try to understand!"

Sandy focused on Thomas but did not reply. It was fairly obvious to Thomas that the surface problem stemmed from Sandy's insecurity and lack of self-esteem that caused her to develop the annoying practice of "accusatory requests" that Bob could not handle. A professional psychologist might start a lengthy therapy treatment to control this insecurity, but, Thomas was not a professional psychologist and he believed in the basic philosophy that perfection could not be reached in this life, and that the best solution to most conflicts was "simplified psychoanalysis," which to him meant to expose the surface problem and help the patient adjust behavior to effect peaceful co-existence.

Thomas put his hand on Sandy's and started in a fatherly tone, "This is a basic case of what we call an accusatory request. It is a rather common practice that can get out of hand. You are not completely comfortable in asking Bob to do little favors for you, and you may even feel that he should do these favors for you without asking; so you make your requests in a defensive manor with what we call an accusatory request. You try to build a case that you are deserving of the favor and your partner should not refuse you. In so doing, you make accusations that the partner has in some way or another not treated you rightly! Your partner, who nearly always tries to please you, takes offense and tries to defend himself. If you simply make a request and indicate that you would like a favor, I don't think that you would ever be refused, and I don't believe that you would have to listen to a defense, because there would be no defense necessary. You might feel an obligation to later on do something in return, but that's the way it should be anyway, isn't it? Each meeting the needs of each other."

"Why is it always my fault?" Sandy dejectedly questioned.

Short Stories and Tall Tales　　19

"It isn't a batter of blame," Thomas countered, "It's a matter of adjustment. Simply change that particular behavior pattern and I believe that you will solve the problem."

Sandy wasn't completely comfortable accepting the fact that she may have been the cause of the conflict with Bob, but she decided that she would give Thomas's advice a try.

Thomas had several meetings with his two parishioners, and to his amazement, he was extremely successful in getting the two back together again.

Counseling isn't so tough after all, he thought. All you need to do is keep your head and use common sense. The best advise of all is to just listen. Nine times out of ten, the ones being counseled solve their own problems.

The teenagers in the parish also came to look upon Thomas as their problem solver as well. There were certain things that many of them just could not discuss with their parents, and Thomas was their salvation. The number one problem was sex!

"I actually do not want to have sex with every boy I go out with," many of the girls confided, "But if I don't, nobody will go out with me!"

Thomas didn't take the customary approach with this issue and give the girls a motivational speech on virtue and honor. Instead, he established group sessions with both girls and boys together after first having sessions with boys in which he emphasized the needs and desires of young ladies and sessions with girls emphasizing the needs and desires of young men.

In the group sessions, he proposed a mature, responsible approach to developing relationships.

"It is the insecure and emotionally inadequate person, male or female, that must have sex as the basis for their relationships," he would explain. "A boy who has respect for a girl would not think of violating her, and a girl worthy of respect would not stay in a relationship with a boy that did not respect her."

"Teenagers and young adults need companionship and affection," he would also tell them, "But, companionship and affection without respect is not a relationship worth keeping. Wait until you're married before you take the responsibility of having children. It works out a lot better that way."

Most understood and welcomed the guidelines that Thomas had set for them. Some, however, needed special counseling, and some had to be salvaged from their mistakes. In the next couple of years, Father Thomas O'Finnigan McDonough became known as the "Social Adjustment Counselor."

"Emotional misunderstandings are the root of most domestic problems," he often told his flock. " I try to help change priorities from acquiring things to establishing relationships. Once this priority is accepted, amazing and wonderful things happen to the parties involved."

Thomas felt it necessary to point out, "Conflict brought about by perceived injustice is the most serious and most difficult to resolve. In these cases, counseling is needed for both the victim and the perpetrator. The time to counsel this type of conflict is in early childhood before it festers into violence. Bullies and those who ridicule and ostracize others initiate behavior reaction that can open wounds that may erupt in later life resulting in tragic violence."

He was particularly good with the youth and he was the driving force that provided a city-wide youth sports program where trophies were given for 'sportsmanship' instead of winning.

In spite of his enormous success, there were times when Thomas was absolutely stumped. When two women approached him to perform a wedding ceremony for them; such was the case.

"What do you do with a conservative Bishop and a liberal congregation?" he pondered. As it turned out, all of the congregation wasn't all that liberal; and following the lead of the Bishop wasn't as difficult as he had thought. But what about his inner self? He hadn't become a Priest to please the Bishop or his congregation either. He had become a Priest to please God; and pleasing God meant to obey God's laws and to minister to 'the least of these my brethren.'

Thomas was not a Priest to stand in judgment, he was a Priest to uphold the 'Word of God.' Were the words of a liberal Bishop the words of God? What about the words of a conservative Bishop? Even the Pope has now declared that some previous infallible decisions were fallible.

"We all have a direct link to God through prayer," Thomas thought. The answer is to pray until you receive an answer.

Thomas became deeply concerned with the problem of officially condoning a homosexual relationship; and after several weeks had gone by without an answer to his prayers, he called in the two young women to pray with him.

Both women were professionals, one an attorney and one a psychologist. The attorney had been raised by her grandparents and was quiet and refined. The psychologist had a most difficult time with a domineering husband and a totally mixed up son that was bi-sexual. She was a bit sloppy, somewhat overweight, and quite a contrast to the trim attorney. However they both were classical music buffs and seemed to be most compatible.

The ladies were absolutely bewildered by Thomas' action; but they went along with the Priest basically out of curiosity. After a couple of prayer sessions, the women embraced Thomas and decided that it wasn't necessary

Short Stories and Tall Tales

to have a formal wedding, and if they could attend church and follow their own conscience in the practice of their faith, they were satisfied.

Thomas wasn't completely comfortable with this solution even though, on the surface, the problem was solved. In his heart, he knew that the 'problem' was not solved at all but he decided to let the matter lie.

Life went on rather smoothly in the St. Thomas Parish for nearly a year, when one day, two gay men approached Thomas to perform a 'commitment ceremony' for them. His unsolved problem of nearly a year ago emerged again, bigger than ever.

One of the men had had several partners in the past and was looked upon with disgust by almost everyone in the Parish. His new partner was sheepish and a pitiful sight in Thomas' eyes. He felt that he could refuse the ceremony on the grounds of a morality issue separate and apart from homosexuality. But, Thomas had to be honest with himself. There was a deeper problem that he had to face and it was not his nature to "cop out."

When Thomas went to the next vestry meeting, Thomas brought up the issue of the Church's stand on homosexuality with his Senior Warden. He was shocked when he discovered that there was a large number of homosexuals in his own congregation, including two on the vestry itself. It seemed to Thomas that his world was coming apart. Had what he learned and believed all his life not the truth? He decided that this would have to be the topic for their weekly Bible Study, and it would continue as the topic until he found some answers that he could accept.

Chapter VI - Examining the Problem

Bible study turned out to be enlightening chaos. Everyone had an opinion even though it was several sessions before they began to express it. Two things were apparent; First, that almost everyone believed that Freedom was their most cherished , God Given right; and Second, that no one in the entire congregation truly understood about homosexuality.

George Smith, a well decorated veteran and self-styled macho man stood up and boldly stated," I earned my right to freedom, and I say that I have the right to do what I please with my body."

An avowed lesbian stood up and answered in a sarcastic smirk, "Freedom is a gift, and it's given to all of us."

The Senior Warden, without doubt the most pompous and proper person in the parish, stood up with his hands out stretched for silence and attention.

"Freedom is a responsibility," he eloquently stated.

After about two seconds of respectful pause, bedlam brook loose.

"I worked in a factory making tanks for the Army and I feel I have the right to do as I please too," a nervous voice blurted out.

George Smith recognized the voice as belonging to what he called a 'draft dodger,' and he just had to retaliate; "And you made more money than you ever did in your life."

Thomas felt that it was about time to step in and shouted, "Order! Order! Yes, Freedom is a gift, and it is a responsibility; and we thank all who help to preserve it."

Thomas noted frustration and anger on the face of George and a couple of other respected Veterans, then quickly continued, "Of course, we have a special gratitude for those who gave their lives for freedom." This seemed to quiet the group and Thomas seized upon the opportunity to get back to the issue they were studying.

"Personal Freedom, is of course a valid consideration in the approach to homosexuality. However, I submit that homosexuality can not be accepted or condoned on the basis of freedom alone. We must first understand what homosexuality is and then consider what the Bible has to say about it."

Mingled shouts came from all directions. "We all know that it is unnatural and against God's Law."

"Who said so?"

"The Flaming Fags are a disgrace!"

"The disgrace is your own ignorance."

Soon, it was just noise and it was impossible to determine what anyone was saying.

"Order! Order!" shouted Thomas. As the noise settled, the Senior Warden again stretched out his hands for attention and offered, "Father Thomas! Why don't you give us some words of wisdom to help us better understand just what this is all about."

Thomas did not want to make an official statement on the issue because he knew that there were many different opinions on the subject, and even the Bishops themselves did not agree with each other. He had hoped that they would evolve a solution through readings from the Bible and some objective discussion. However, he was now on the spot; he had no choice.

"Let me get some notes together, and I'll make a presentation at our next meeting."

"Why wait until our next meeting?" the Junior Warden interrupted, "Why not make it a topic for your sermon this coming Sunday?"

There was dead silence; then it appeared that there was near unanimous approval. Thomas wasn't quite sure what he had said in reply, but it seemed that everyone understood that he had accepted the challenge.

Bible Study was held on Thursday night, and by Friday noon, several parishioners had slowly walked by the church. They were surreptitiously looking at the Church Sign that gave the title of the coming Sunday's sermon. More came by Friday evening, and by Saturday noon, almost the entire vestry had been past. Finally, at 5 PM on Saturday, Thomas posted the topic for his sermon.

"He, She, Him and Her."

The word spread like wild fire. Curiosity was intense and even spread beyond the congregation itself. On Sunday morning the Church was packed with people standing in the back. Several people walking by, with no knowledge of what the sermon was about, crowded in just to see what was going on.

For the first time in his life, Thomas had stage fright. He had prepared his topic well, but he was not ready to present his thoughts as the direct word from God. Actually, there was very little Biblical reference in his sermon. For the most part it was his own thoughts even though he had prayed about it and felt that it was what God wanted him to say.

During the opening prayers and beginning liturgy, Thomas began to regain his composure; and when it was time for the sermon, he was reasonably ready to deliver what he felt might be the last time he would speak at St. Thomas Church.

Thomas cleared his throat and slowly started his dissertation.

"In our interdependent society, happiness and success depend to a great degree upon the establishment of compatible, working relationships. Relationships between parents and children, husband and wife, neighbors and friends, customers and businesses, employer and employee, and buyer and seller, to name a few. Almost all activity in the society involves interaction between individuals and/or groups of individuals. Poor relationships lead to disappointment, failure and sometimes violence. Studies have shown that the greatest cause for failure in the work place is the inability to get along with fellow workers.

Divorce, in what was once considered a sacred relationship between a man and a woman, has become commonplace. Child abuse is a national disgrace.

There are many reasons for developing relationships. Almost all of us have a need and desire to establish close ties with others. One of the major drives requiring the development of a relationship is sex. Unfortunately this drive has resulted in some of the most confused, abused and misused relationships that have ever evolved. It is this topic that I am going to address this morning.

Sex is a divine gift from God. It allows us to participate in his miracle of Creation.

Sex is the source of our greatest joy; a son or a daughter. Sex gives us our greatest responsibility in this life; the propagation of the human race to serve and obey our creator.

If you do not recognize that children are our greatest joy; and that guiding these children into responsible, caring adults is our greatest responsibility in this life, I suggest that you have lost sight of the true meaning of life; and that you have fallen victim to the evils of selfishness and materialism.

Sex is three dimensional; physical, psychological and spiritual. Sexual relationships therefore must be three dimensional as well.

To treat sex as merely a physical function is as foolish as describing happiness as wealth. I am going to attempt to give an objective overview of the issues involved, and to present some suggested guidelines for the understanding and development of compatible, unobtrusive sexual relationships. Every attempt has been made to eliminate professional and technical terminology, and to present issues and concepts in simple, understandable language.

I have chosen the title for this sermon, 'He, She, Him and Her.' Perhaps the best way to start a discussion on sexual relationships is to clarify sexual terminology. Our society has developed a myriad of definitions for sex, a number of which could be universally acceptable.

In the simplest and most accurate terms, sex is the propagation of the species. In the 60's and 70's there was a great movement among many of the youth to determine 'who we are.' In the 80's and 90's the question seemed to be 'what we are.'

Literally thousands of people are 'coming out of the closet' so to speak, and they are declaring themselves to be 'homosexuals.' Many of these people do not fully understand their own identity; or their place in society. They only know that they have special interests, and that they want their share of the "American Dream;' to pursue their own interests.

The term 'homosexual' itself is confusing. A simple switch to the classification of 'Gender' could lead to a clearer understanding of their goals and identity. The confused concept of the word 'sex' may perhaps be at the heart of this confusion. The word sex has been used as a synonym for love, gender, intercourse, foreplay, sodomy, masturbation and a few other less acceptable words. It denotes a specific style of advertisement, dress, talk, look, expression, and what have you. From a word that was whispered in secrecy a few decades ago, it has become one of the most used words in our vocabulary today.

Sex might more accurately be defined as procreation; the sex act as intercourse; the gender that fertilizes the egg as the male; the gender that carries the egg as the female; and the genders that do not procreate, the Gay and the Lesbian. Those quasi-sex acts that stimulate and relieve procreative instincts could be grouped under the general heading of masturbation. The quasi-sex acts would include all except intercourse.

Masturbation is a common practice for all four genders with a very wide variation of categories.

Love is an unconditional commitment that does not necessarily involve sex at all.

Such clarification might possibly play havoc with the advertising industry, but this might be justice for the havoc that the advertising industry has caused with our misconception of sex.

The first form of relief for the pent-up sex drive is generally the pursuit of the opposite gender. Often this pursuit is thwarted and masturbation becomes the means to relieve this powerful drive.

Short Stories and Tall Tales   27

As a person matures, the natural development is to a heterosexual relationship. There are many things that happen in life to impede and change what we generally call a natural development, but that is another topic in itself. One of the current problems in society today, and the topic of today's lesson, is the establishment of a compatible Christian approach to all of the evolved sexual relationships, the Gays, the Lesbians and the Heterosexuals.

In our society personal freedom is the basis of our culture. In order to have personal freedom we must respect and protect the personal freedom of everyone else. To accomplish this we must accept the restrictions that preserve personal freedom.

First and foremost, we must respect the personal privacy of others. We can not just tolerate, we must respect this privacy. And, each individual must respect their own privacy. If two people are in love (or committed to each other) and wish to have a lasting relationship with each other, regardless of their gender, we must respect that relationship. And, I must add, the two people committed to each other must respect their own relationship as well. It is clearly stated in God's Word that sodomy is a sin against God and man. But we have no right to assume that two persons of the same sex who are living together are guilty of this sin! We have laws to protect the rights of both parties in a "heterogender" relationship. The primary concern is that one member of the relationship does not take advantage of and infringe upon the rights of the other member in the relationship.

The law says that both parties must be of legal age, for example and both parties must submit to the dictates of the court if they wish to dissolve their relationship. We don't seem to have any firmly established laws to govern "homogender" relationships, and perhaps this is one of the major reasons for the problems evolving in this area.

A simple solution might be the recognition of "heterogender" relationship laws in.regard.to homogender relationships! We do not concern ourselves with the personal, private activities of married couples unless society suspects that a member of that relationship is being denied their legal rights. Perhaps the same concern should be given to homogender relationships. I can not speak for all of Christianity, but this is the policy that I plan to follow in governing the activities of this parish; and I believe that God will approve and bless our actions."

Thomas awkwardly backed away form the pulpit and sat in this chair. There was complete silence through out the church, not even breathing could be heard. There was neither a sign of approval or rejection.

"I hope this is a dream," Thomas said to himself as he waited for something,—anything, to happen. Finally, after what seemed like ages, the Choir Director nodded to the Senior Warden who sang in the choir, and sat in the front row of course, who in turn nodded to his wife who sat in her rightful place in the first seat of the first row on the right hand side of the main isle. The Senior Warden's Wife nodded to Thomas who almost jumped out of his chair and he in turn nodded to the Choir Director. The next thing that Thomas could remember was following the procession down the isle and retiring to the church parlors for coffee hour. He did recall that there seemed to be very little singing coming from such a large group, but he had no idea of how his message was received. Anticipating the worst, Thomas contemplated his retirement sermon for next Sunday.

The Church Parlor seemed to be nearly as crowded as the Church had been, but only a few of the people actually drank any of the coffee or ate any of the delicious sweets that the ladies of the church took pride in and provided every Sunday. It seemed to Thomas like everyone was standing around gawking at him. After a fashion, the Junior Warden approached Thomas with a cup of coffee in one hand, half a pastry in the other hand, and half a pastry in his mouth. Thomas wasn't sure of just what the warden was trying to say, but it sounded like he said, "I hope you don't look upon my relationship with my partner as masturbation!"

Thomas was noticeably disturbed that the message he had so carefully prepared was reduced to this minuscule thought.

"I had thought of your relationship as more of a commitment," he said in a rather defensive tone.

"Of course, of course," the warden's half full mouth responded.

There was an awkward silence, then Thomas broke in with, "I wish some one would say something; anything at all would be better than this silence." Little did he realize that in less than 24 hours, he would welcome silence.

"I think that you will be hearing something soon," the warden offered, "Charlotte Applebee (Social Editor of the local paper) was in church and left right after the service ended."

Thomas turned a deathly shade of white and began to feel a bit ill. There was small talk during the rest of the hour with several groups of parishioners but still not approval or rejection. One thing seemed quite clear however, many were looking forward to the next Study Session. It didn't seem right to call it Bible Study, as they really didn't discuss the Bible. However, Thomas made every effort to follow Biblical teachings in every discussion they had, and he felt that his message from the pulpit was completely compatible with the teaching of Jesus; also, that it was within acceptable moral standards.

When Mrs. Murphy, the housekeeper, served breakfast on Monday morning there was something conspicuously missing.

"Where is the morning paper?" Thomas asked.

Short Stories and Tall Tales   29

At first, Mrs. Murphy tried to pretend that she didn't hear him, but then she realized that she wasn't going to get away with that, so she hesitatingly responded, "It must be coming late today."

Just as Thomas finished breakfast, Mrs. Murphy handed him the paper and quickly walked away. The headlines of the local section stated, "ST. THOMAS CHURCH ADOPTS POLICY TO SUPPORT HOMOSEXUALS"

The article went on to cite "The Reverend Thomas O'Finnigan McDonough takes a bold stand to perform Homosexual marriages."

Before Thomas could finish reading the article, Mrs. Murphy entered the room and announced, "The Bishop is on the phone and he wants to speak with you right away!" Thomas took a deep sigh and picked up the phone.

"Thomas here!"

"Thomas, this is the Bishop. I have just read the morning paper. Please tell me that there is some mistake!"

Thomas took a quick breath, then answered, "I haven't finished reading the paper yet."

The Bishop quickly interjected, "Well Thomas, I must tell you that Church Law isn't made by Priests in small churches; It is made by Bishops in a formal procedure that was established centuries ago."

The Bishop's reaction disturbed Thomas, then he felt anger. He hadn't established Church Law, he had responded to a neglected problem in caring for his "sheep." This is America, he reasoned; the land of freedom and free speech. He didn't become a Priest to become a puppet for a Bishop or anyone else. His allegiance is to God, and he is doing God's will to the best of his ability.

Thomas collected his thoughts, took another deep breath, then calmly stated, "As I said, Bishop, I haven't finished reading the article yet. Perhaps I should finish the article and get back to you later." With that he wished the Bishop a 'Good Day' and hung up.

Thomas got his coat and hat and walked to the kitchen. "I'm going out, Mrs. Murphy, and don't answer the phone. Let the answering machine get it. I'll call you if I'm going to be back for dinner.

Thomas spent the next few days conferring with selected parishioners that he felt would give him a good idea of how his flock had taken his sermon.

The general thinking in the homosexual community was that it was a major step to have rules for their commitment just as there were for the Marriage Commitment. However the feeling was also expressed that his emphasis on personal privacy would put them back into the closet again. One of the vestrymen repeated the time worn expression, "The more things change, the more they stay the same."

The consensus in the 'straight' community was a little more encouraging. Almost everyone felt that they understood 'the genders' a little better now, and with that understanding came a greater tolerance if not complete acceptance. Later when he got the groups together, however, it seemed to be a different story. Heated emotions broke out a couple of times early in the discussions, and Thomas had to use maximum diplomacy to keep order. It appeared that when in the presence of other members of their own community, both groups felt that they had to defend what they thought the other members in their group believed. Thomas reasoned that this was an attempt to maintain the respect and approval of their own group. "Break down this 'Peer Pressure Syndrome' and real progress might be made," he thought.

When order had been restored for the third time, a most provoking question was asked, "Should the couple in the 'non productive gender' be allowed to adopt children?"

"Certainly not," came back an immediate reply from the floor. "If a couple chooses to enter into a non productive relationship, they have no right to the children of a productive relationship."

Hardly before the reply was ended, another parishioner blurted out, "What about those barren couples in a 'productive' relationship that adopt children?"

Several people started talking at once. The dominant voice shouted, "You are never satisfied until you take away our rights and make us second class citizens!"

Thomas could see that emotions were erupting again and called for order. A vestryman who was a prominent attorney in the city raised his hand for recognition. Thomas was eager to have a calm, respected voice about this time, and recognized the speaker.

"The issue we are talking about here is not individual rights, but community rights. The rights to be protected in this case are the rights of the child involved. Under the law, the child belongs to the State. State Laws are total community laws protecting both individual rights and community rights. Since the child is the ward of the State, the State determines the child's rights which reflects the moral judgment of the majority of the citizens in the State."

Everyone did not buy the attorney's legalize, but it did appear to calm emotions for the moment. One of the wardens who was a recognized leader in the gay community stood up to gain attention and calmly orated, "I can understand the opposition to the adoption of the products of the heterosexual community by the gay community, but I cannot tolerate the opposition for duly qualified members of the gay community to become Priests and school teachers,—and government officials. Gay persons in these positions would

Short Stories and Tall Tales   31

be no more influential to unduly promote their life styles than a heterosexual person would be to unduly promote theirs. We, in the gay community, do not want to be tolerated, we want to be accepted for what we are. Some of the worlds greatest artists and proven leaders have been from the gay community."

There was a round of applause quite obviously coming from the gay community members, but there were several noticeable supporters from the heterosexual community as well.

After things had settled down a bit, a young lady who had not spoken before at any of the meetings nervously addressed Thomas.

"I recognize many of our gifted homosexual people, but I also recognize, and am fearful of the ones who use their positions to commit terrible crimes such as the Priest who molests young altar boys."

Again bedlam broke loose. The loudest voice came forth before Thomas could call for order and shouted, "Madam, you are talking about pedophiles, not homosexuals; and they are as disgusting to the gay community as they are to the heterosexual community."

Again, before Thomas could respond, as he deeply felt he should in support of this point, another voice blurted out, "Its the blatant promiscuity of the gay community that I object to!"

Strangely enough, there wasn't a major response to this charge, but the man with the loud voice that had answered the last charge stood up to address the issue.

"Again let me enlighten you. The responsible members of the gay community are as embarrassed and concerned about promiscuity in both communities as you are. There is fully as much irresponsible infidelity in the heterosexual community as their is in the gay community, and you think nothing of it. Some of the highest ranking government officials in our country, and from the heterosexual community I might add, have been found guilty of deviant sex acts, and the public condones it."

A vestryman who was also the local chairman of one of the major political parties stood up to respond. "I understand what you are saying, but I don't think the public has condoned the promiscuity of its leaders; I believe that they are simply calling for a punishment that fits the crime."

Thomas felt that it was time to step in. "I think we are getting a little off the track. I do feel that we have aired a number of vital concerns and although we haven't solved the major problems by any means, we have been given some food for thought that should result in greater understanding."

"Actually," Thomas continued, "We will never solve all of our problems in this world. Perhaps the best we can do is try to get along and treat each other with Christian Charity."

A respected member of the Vestry stood up to get attention. "One last thought," he started. "You spoke of the sin of sodomy in your sermon, and also that we should not assume anyone guilty of sodomy just because they are committed to someone of the same gender; but what about the person who blatantly defends the practice of sodomy?"

Thomas was sure that this question would be asked sooner or later and was ready with an answer. "To be sure, there is no leadership position in the Church for anyone who advocates the practice of any sinful act, but there is certainly a place in the membership of the church for such a person. The Church is made up of sinners for we are all sinners and fall short of the glory of God. The Church is the place where all can come in peace and love to find their way to the Alter of God. As members of the Church, it is our duty to treat each other with love and compassion."

Just then Thomas noticed the Bishop sitting unobtrusively in the back and it suddenly occurred to him that this might be a good time to end the study group.

At the close of the meeting, the Bishop came forward to speak with Thomas; "I think that I was a little hard on you, Thomas. I felt that you had opened up a can of worms, but sometimes I guess the can just has to be opened. Thomas was startled, but pleased.

The two retired to the Rectory where Mrs. Murphy served them coffee and some of her famous pastries. After Thomas and the Bishop had finished small talk and formalities, the mood changed to serious discussion.

"You know, Thomas, given the human need for companionship and the threatening incidents of date rape and domestic abuse; were I born a woman, I might very well have become a lesbian my self. The answer is not to judge and condemn for it is written, 'Judge Not!' The answer is to develop a community of unconditional love where all can live in peace and harmony as God willed us to do. Christian principles should be presented in love, not as threats with punishment of hell. We have to love one another as God has loved us."

Thomas interjected, "But Bishop, there are so many conflicting interpretations. If we take every verse literally, we can easily end up disagreeing with ourselves."

"I have to agree, Thomas," the Bishop continued; "One can really get caught up in focusing upon the 'Letter of the Law.' There are many things in the Bible that seem to be contradictory when taken separately at face value. I believe that is God telling us that some concepts are beyond human language.

There are times when we have to pray and be led to the 'Spirit of the Law.' The reason we have so many problems with the civil law is the obsession that the Constitution is the perfect source to solve all problems. Attorneys, using

Short Stories and Tall Tales 33

human logic and brilliance, focus on the letter of the law and try to make it work for their benefit. Right or wrong isn't even a consideration; its simply win or lose. The advantage we have is prayer. The Bible tells us that when two or more people are gathered together in My Name, there will I be also.

I know that you prayed with your Parish, and I am sure that God was with you; but, Thomas, next time you want to consider Church Law, could you kindly include me in your prayer group?"

Thomas remembered the time he sought the Bishop's counsel on divorce and he was told to proceed as way opened; but he didn't think that this was something that he should confront the Bishop with at this time.

"I would welcome your prayers, Bishop," he finally spoke out. "We haven't actually formulated any concrete policies at this point. Perhaps we could develop some acceptable guidelines for homogender relationships. The Bishop closed his eyes and appeared to be in deep, troubled thought, then said, "No Thomas, I don't think that would be the way to go. I rather think that we should come up with some rules for a relationship of commitment that could govern any personal relationship that was a serious involvement. These policies could then be applied to each individual case."

Thomas sensed that there was a bit of politics involved in the Bishop's suggestion, but, another word for politics could be diplomacy; and there certainly isn't anything wrong with diplomacy. Perhaps diplomacy is one product of prayer.

"Marriage would remain a traditional commitment, then," Thomas asserted; "And any other commitment would be an act of its own – sanctioned by a special Commitment Sacrament?" Thomas's assertion definitely ended in a questioning tone, and the Bishop was quick to respond accordingly,

"A Sacrament? Perhaps this is an area that should be considered in prayer. As you said in your closing remarks at the study session, we will never solve all of the problems in this world, but if we pray and follow God's will we can develop better relationships that are honorable and honest."

Thomas could see that the development of harmonious relationships was the basis for solving many of our major problems including divorce as well as sexual and racial discrimination. But how does one go about developing good relationships? Obviously, this should be started in the training of children.

After quick consideration of these thoughts, Thomas questioned the Bishop, "Shouldn't all of this be part of our Religious Education Program?" The Bishop pondered the thought for a moment, then responded.

"You know Thomas, in our society where the emphasis is on earning a living, we spend too little time on learning how to live."

Thomas was excited and interjected before the Bishop could continue his thought; "Our society has changed over the years to the point where children learn more about establishing relationships from their peers than they do from their parents. Perhaps the Church has not been involved in the education of our youth as it should have been."

After a brief pause, Thomas continued, "Perhaps the training for establishing relationships, particularly relationships relating to marriage and families, is the responsibility of the Church and not the Public Schools.

"I think that you are right Thomas," The Bishop broke in. "I am going to set up an Executive Committee to examine our religious education curriculum and come up with some effective means to guide our children in the establishment of good relationships. There is much in the Bible relating to this, but it must be presented in today's language for today's community."

The Bishop paused again for a moment, then turned to Thomas. "I'm going to ask you to head up that committee and to select some members from your parish to serve with you. I will also select a number of people from the other parishes. This is an activity that is long overdo. I'm counting on you, Thomas."

Thomas was pleased. He felt like an astronaut. He had helped to take one giant step for mankind,—Or perhaps just one small step! At least it was a step.

CHAPTER VII - RESEARCHING THE PROBLEM

The Bishop had set the date for the committee meeting on the first Wednesday of the following month. This was only three weeks away and Thomas started preparations immediately.

"The first thing to do is to define our goal or objective," Thomas reasoned. He knew what he wanted to accomplish, but to phrase the objective in completely understandable and acceptable terms was not as easy as it might seem.

"To develop a curriculum that could be used in Religious Education that would help people to get along with each other?" was the result of the first hour of searching.

"Too long," he decided. How about something simple like, "To develop Christian Relationships?"

Perhaps this was too simple to have meaning for the average person," he pondered

Thomas then wisely decided to do some research in the Library before coming up with objectives or anything else. After a week of pouring through volumes of religious and philosophical writing, he came across the doctoral dissertation of an obscure little college professor entitled, "Relationships and Responsibilities."

This seemed to be basically just what he was looking for. The more he read, the more he could relate to the writing. Thomas copied down parts of the dissertation to present to the Committee.

"Educators have long realized that the three R's of Reading, Riting and Rithmatic need to be supplemented by the three R's of Reason, Respect and Responsibility to prepare students to become peaceful co-existors in our society today.. However, unlike Reading, Riting & Rithmatic, we have little or no curriculum to guide teachers in helping students learn these other three R's!

As in Sex Education, learning about reason, respect and responsibility does not always come automatically and naturally through life experiences. We must come up with a curriculum that will guide children through a presentation of the basic concepts of the other three R's to give them the chance to develop positive learning in this vital area. It should be our goal for children to become functional and productive without learning the 'hard way' by making mistakes that may leave scars and prevent fulfillment, Thomas reasoned.

Thomas then ran across a pertinent introduction for a course of study:

MAINTAINING A SOCIETY..

A Society is an organization of individuals who have joined together for the good of all of the individuals in the Society. Each person in the society has his or her unique contribution to the society, which in effect, is the consideration of the welfare of the other individuals in the society. The basic concept for the society is that with each individual contributing to the welfare of the other individuals in the society, the welfare of the society and the welfare of every individual in the society is enhanced. The ability to peacefully co-exist with the other members in the society is a skill that every member of the society must possess! The acquisition of these skills is the responsibility of every individual in the society. The TEACHING of these skills is the responsibility of the Parents and the Society itself. The development of RELATIONSHIPS between individuals that will provide for peaceful co-existence is a monumental task. Guidance and instruction for developing Relationships must be given from birth. Traditionally, Parents, with the help of the 'Church' were given the responsibility for early child development. It was thought that a child's character was pretty well established by the age of seven when the child was required to attend school. This was based upon the tradition of a strong family in which the Mother was the main 'full time' participant. With working mothers being the rule rather than the exception, there is a void that must be filled. As it stands at the present, many think that this void must be filled by the public schools. Unfortunately the public schools are forbidden to teach morals and religious beliefs. It is unfortunate because good relationships are based upon good morals and good religious beliefs. Consequently, the teaching of Relationships in the pubic schools has been neglected.

An other avenue to teach Relationships is through the written word. Fortunately, there is still freedom to express the written word and therefore a book on Relationships is in order.

Thomas also copied down parts of other dissertations on the same topic that he thought might be helpful.

THE FIRST RULE OF A HARMONOUS RELATIONSHIP

"Always look for the best." Almost everything said or expressed can be taken two ways – positively and negatively. If you take everything said in a positive way, always looking for the best, you will never be guilty of taking anything the 'wrong way.'

DEVELOPING A FRIENDSHIP

The greatest gain in life is the development of a friendship. It is wonderful to have friendly relationships with all acquaintances, but to have a true friendship with another person is the greatest gift that one can ever have. A friend is your confidant; your support; a source of comfort in time of need; a source of joy when administering to their needs. In order to have a friend, you must be a friend. A friend never divulges any private or intimate feelings that you have been privileged to share with that friend to any other person; and that includes another friend if you are lucky enough to have more than one friend. At times, this may become a tremendously difficult task. Gossiping is one of life's greatest temptations, and sharing deep secrets with a friend is one of the greatest treasures of friendship.

Mastering the art of being a friend is a most difficult task to achieve. Mastering the art of being a friend to more than one person is geometrically more difficult. Most successful multiple friendships are "group friendships' such as the fictional 'Three Musketeers. 'Having more than one friend is not impossible, it just requires greater effort and greater self-discipline.

CHOOSING A SPOUSE

The second most intimate relationship in our society is the relationship of marriage. (The first is parent/child) Only best friends should enter into this vital relationship. Many marriage relationships are entered into based almost solely on sexual compatibility.

As important as sexual compatibility is to a marriage, it must take second place to friendship. Sex is highly over rated in our society and quite often it becomes an obsession. Sex is a natural drive that can result in a momentarily exciting experience with almost anyone and/or anything. The purpose of sex is to procreate. The responsibility of procreation is perhaps the greatest responsibility of this life. Part of that responsibility is to help the development of the ability to create harmonious relationships among the future generations.

Of course, Thomas didn't agree with everything, but this was the kind of information that he was looking for! Unfortunately, there were no Biblical references; and you could hardly have a religious education program devoid of Biblical references. Thomas felt sure that what he had read was basically compatible with the teaching of Christ, and he spent the next week pouring through the Bible in an attempt to find references that he could quote to support or refute this text.

"Do unto others as you would have them do unto you!" Have the same concern and consideration for others as you have for yourself.

This is the Golden Rule. Almost everyone believes in it, but not that many actually follow the rule. This, simply stated is our problem. ""How do we make people follow the Golden Rule; or rather, how do we influence people to follow the Golden Rule. Perhaps by following the Golden Rule ourselves?

"But wait!" Thomas paused for a moment. "There is something that I have overlooked. The first commandment demanded a total commitment to God Almighty. We must first develop our relationship with God, then we can work on our relationships with others."

The library research had some excellent thoughts, but without a commitment to the Almighty, we exist on a meaningless level that ends after a short life-time. If we focus entirely on the human level, we can expect most people to become competitive and selfish. Our goal on the human level becomes a matter of using and exploiting our neighbor or anyone else for our own welfare; and this is hardly loving your neighbor as ourselves.

Thomas spent the next few days in prayer. He desperately wanted to come up with a miracle; an answer that would be compatible with American Freedom and the American Way of Life,— and also promote unselfish love for others. To have a society that loved their neighbor as themselves.

In spite of Thomas' prayers, no answer was received. When time came for the first meeting of the Committee, he still felt unprepared. He related to the committee his readings, and his experience of trying to come up with some sort of an agenda for their discussion. He suggested that they all bow in silent prayer until God gave someone a message.

Short Stories and Tall Tales   39

The silence went on for what seemed like hours, then the room filled with intense anxiety. As the mood evolved into an unresisting submission to the will of God.

The Bishop stood up and began to speak. "Brethren, God gave us the answer roughly two thousand years ago. He told us through his son, "Seek ye first the Kingdom of Heaven and its righteousness, and all things shall be added unto you."

The message was given again to Thomas when the Spirit told him that the first relationship we must establish is the one with God Almighty. We can work to help build this divine relationship as the Church was established to do, or we can foolishly search for a way to make our will God's Will.

Prayer, meditation, and study sessions such as those conducted at St. Thomas Church all help to reach our goals in this life, but nothing good or lasting will ever be accomplished until we first develop our relationship with God."

The Committee concentrated on renewing their faith, and worked hard to try to fulfill God's Will.

Chapter VIII - The Committee at Work

There was great enthusiasm as the Committee prepared draft after draft trying to come up with a program that would be acceptable to all but as time went by, the enthusiasm waned and the feeling of helplessness and defeat began to take over. Finally, after Thomas had called the meeting to order, one of the vestrymen, a retired college professor, stood up to be recognized and Thomas gave him the floor.

"Thomas," he started, " You have done a great job of researching and enlightening us on the issues; but it seems to me that we are restricted in our thinking to solve the problems by traditions. We can't possibly solve any problems by doing things the way we did that gave us the problems that we have!

Bear with me for just a moment and consider the problems we face. There is a natural sex drive that starts for most in their early teens. Our traditions, which we enforce as divine rules of conduct, require complete abstinence from the fulfillment of this drive until around the mid twenties when most people get married today. As a result, there is mass frustration for about ten years during the time when this drive is at its height.

Why not use today's means to deal with today's problem and advocate safe sex and birth control practices?"

There was considerable unrest in the room and all eyes were on Thomas to counter this heathen approach.

Thomas started slowly and cautiously, "It is true that times have changed, and that many of our rules of conduct are man made extensions of rules rather than commandments from God. However, we cannot discard centuries of wisdom in an attempt to solve our problems.

Another voice broke in, "We're not trying to discard wisdom, we're trying to make life bearable. Very few people actually follow these strict rules anyway."

Another person jumped to his feet and added, "My son countered my attempt to enforce the rules with 'Your rules simply force kids to masturbate!"

Several of the committee members exhibited shock at such distasteful talk, but no one registered disagreement. Quickly, Thomas rose to the occasion.

"Masturbation has been quietly accepted as an unrecognized alternative to heterosexual activity among the youth by perhaps a large majority of our people, and many feel that it may be a valid temporary answer, but it does have some serious consequences. Some say that it promotes homosexual activity, and most professionals dealing with this subject will tell you that it tends to promote psychological imbalance that often diminishes the maximum development of a healthy heterosexual relationship."

Thomas paused for a moment. He was aware that there were topics discussed that were not welcomed by many of the committee members, but this is the down side of "brainstorming." Perhaps this is the price that must be paid to find valid solutions to problems, but what could he do to make this a little more acceptable to all.

"Let me suggest" he continued, "That we break into small groups for next time and that each group come up with a set of guidelines for sexual conduct to share with the rest of the committee. May I ask you to go wherever you feel led and that you provide a Xerox copy for everyone on the committee. With that the meeting was adjourned.

Thomas' idea was a brilliant success. Each group presented their guidelines and each was respectfully accepted. Thomas studied the proposals during the following week and was ready to act at the next meeting.

Thomas called the meeting to order, "I think that we are all in agreement that Sexual Conduct is the core of one of our biggest issues in society today. We're struggling with pedophiles, rapists, children born out of wedlock, teen pregnancy, homosexuality and disfunctional families, all with sexual relations as the basis of each problem. We have brainstormed and tried to determine the Christian approach to sexual relations. Brainstorming resulted in a rehashing of all of our previous discussions, but finally there was agreement that no problem could ever be solved unless they proceeded with an open mind. In order to correct an existing problem, a change of some sort had to be made, and changes are never made with a closed mind.

It was unanimously agreed that a strong statement should be made that everyone would be tolerant and quietly accept the freedom of others. It was also finally agreed that something should be done to ease the unbearable yoke imposed upon premarital couples. Thomas brought the committee's attention

Short Stories and Tall Tales 43

to the fact that Christ had a compassionate approach to those who felt celibacy was an unbearable yoke and that marriage was acceptable and good. In like manner he proposed, and the committee accepted, the position that premarital sexual relations between consenting adults was acceptable provided that the sanctity of God's gift of creation was observed and respected.

Thomas and the Committee then went a step further and added the rule that once a child had been conceived, divorce was no longer an acceptable option.

Thomas presented the Committee's guidelines to the Church, and although it resulted in some heated discussions, it was accepted not only by St. Thomas Church, but by most Churches in the diocese and many Churches outside of the diocese as well.

Trial marriages became common place, and the number of births out of wedlock drastically receded.. The number of divorces were also greatly reduced. The movement became so popular that several public schools included the "St. Thomas Guidelines" in their sex education program.

This did not last long however as a group advocating separation of Church and State brought legal action and won. Thomas argued to no avail that SEPARATION FROM GOD WAS THE DEFINITION OF HELL!"

The Churches in the Diocese continued to follow Thomas's lead and offered the program on a voluntary basis after school hours. The Religious Education Program plus the weekly Prayer and Study Sessions promoted harmony and fellowship within the Churches involved.

St. Thomas expanded from two Masses on Sunday to five on Sunday and two on Saturday night, all heavily attended. The Church also had one or two community outreach projects going at all times. The "All Year Youth Sports Program" enrolled nearly every young person in the city at one time or another regardless of their church affiliation.

The one thing that pleased Thomas the most was the sincere spirit of brotherly love that enveloped the entire community to a level that was as high as one could possibly expect in this life.

Time finally took its toll on Thomas's tired body, and he passed on to be with Shawn and Teepe and his beloved parents.

One by one, old Church leaders stepped down from their leadership positions to let new members take over the leadership roles.

Gradually, attendance and enthusiasm returned to the level it had been when Thomas first arrived at St. Thomas. St. Thomas then became like most of the other Churches in our society; a physical evidence of the Glory of God, waiting for another Thomas O'Finnigan McDonough to come along and renew the spirit within.

THE RELUCTANT WITNESS

Foreword

There are times in our life when we are called upon to stand up for what we believe in. If you make a promise to the 'Almighty' to be a witness and fail to keep your promise, you may suffer the fate of 'Eric Jones!'

THE RELUCTANT WITNESS is the story of Eric Jones, a young Navy sailor who made a promise to God while in battle in the South Pacific during WWII. Eric was reluctant to keep his promise until——.

The story is based upon a true experience and includes accounts of the desperate Kamikaze assault on the 'Okinawa Picket Line;' the 'Healing' of the occupational forces in Japan after the War; and the influence of a Gideon Testament and a Salvation Army Band in developing a Witness.

Chapter I - Eric Jones Enters the U.S. Navy

It is 1944 and Eric Jones has just turned 17. He was a powerfully built young man with sparkling blond hair that always looked like it had just been washed and set. His boyish face and smooth clear skin invited a woman's caress, but his quiet, serious manor evoked a cautioned approach by both male and female.

Eric's grandmother had signed the necessary papers and he was leaving for boot camp in the U. S. Navy. His single ambition for the past two years had been to join the Navy and defend his country. He had run away from home to join the merchant marines shortly after Pearl Harbor when he was only 15, but that's another story. Now it was legitimate, he was of legal age with his grandmother's blessing, and he was a proud citizen of the country he loved.

Eric had dreamed of being a hero in a naval battle at sea for as long as he could remember. This innocent young man had not seen the bitter, grimy side of war; but his turn would come, and may God be with him.

Eric could hardly contain his emotions. Soon he would be in the thick of the action. His first assignment was boot camp at Sampson Naval Training Station in Western New York on the edge of Seneca Lake.

Seneca Lake was the largest of the New York State Finger Lakes, but it wasn't the ocean and it didn't provide the excitement that Eric was looking for. Nothing was too hard for Eric, he even enjoyed morning calisthenics, an activity that most of the other sailors hated, or at least they all complained as though they hated it. Eric felt a bit superior to the other recruits. He was not haughty or arrogant, but he had served at sea and most of the men in his unit hadn't even seen the ocean. It was evident however that he was an extremely self-confident young man and this did not gain him any close friends.

When Eric finished boot camp, he was ready to go to war. He wanted to be a Gunner's Mate and had signed up for Gunnery School. Like all of the other graduates of the Boot Camp, he impatiently waited for his assignment to be posted on the board.

Finally, on the board, as plain as day - ERIC JONES - SIGNAL SCHOOL.

"What?" he cried, "Are they crazy? " He was a gunner, and a good one. He had proven that. Eric rushed to the Commandant with his complaint.

"Easy Son, Easy! Nearly everyone will be on a gun at general quarters, and when you get to your ship you can request a gunnery position as your battle station. In the meantime, we have to have other skills as well; and right now we need signalmen."

Eric endured his signalman training and was assigned to the LCS (L) 301, scheduled to be commissioned the following month in Portland, Oregon. The train ride across the country took nearly a week, but at last he was on his way to war.

"What is an LCS (L)?" he asked.

"It is a Landing Craft Support Ship," he was told. "It is about 150 feet long, has a crew of 70 men, and has more fire power for its size than a battle ship. It has three 40 MM Anti-Aircraft guns, and four 20 MM Anti-Aircraft guns plus rockets."

The LCS's were designed to go in first on an invasion of a Jap held island; fire its rockets on the beach to wipe out any Jap forces that might be waiting; then beach at intervals to fight off any Jap Aircraft that would try to strafe our troops as they landed on the beaches. This was more like what Eric was looking for. The rockets sounded exciting and he volunteered for the position of Rocket Captain at his very first opportunity.

"Do you know what the Rocket Captain does?" the Gunnery Officer asked him.

"No Sir," he replied.

Well, let me tell you. It isn't hard, but it is dangerous." Eric couldn't have been more pleased. He was shown the rocket launchers which were located just aft of the forward 40 MM Anti-Aircraft gun on the bow. The launchers were little more than 20 welded iron frames that rockets were loaded on to, 10 rockets to a frame. Each rocket was a three foot long 6 ½ pound bomb with a charge attached to the back. At the bottom of the launchers was an electrical device that ignited the charge sending the bomb several hundred feet into the air, dropping down onto the beach ahead. As each rocket fires, the next rocket falls into place against the live electric panel and it in turn fires. This continues until all of the rockets have been sent to the beach.

"As Rocket Captain, you are entrusted with this rocket key plug," the Officer told him. "You supervise the loading of the rocket launchers, making sure that the rockets are all in proper position to fall into place and fire. When

Short Stories and Tall Tales 51

the rockets are ready to fire, you go behind the rocket shield, screw the key into the electrical device there, and phone the Captain that the rockets are ready for launching. When the Captain orders you to launch the rockets, you press the red button next to the key plug and the rockets will fire. After they fire, you go out to the launchers and make sure that all of the rockets have launched. If there are any that have not fired, you have to pick them up and throw them over board as quickly as possible, being careful that they fully clear the side of the ship. One of these babies could blow a hole that would sink the ship. When all is clear, you notify the Captain and you and your crew on the forward 40 take up your positions."

Eric looked puzzled. "Oh yes, I guess I didn't tell you. You will also be Gun Captain of the forward 40 Anti-Aircraft Gun as well. When the rockets are being loaded and until after they are fired, all personnel on the forward part of the ship must vacate that area and your gun crew will be used as rocket loaders. After they load the rockets, they will go aft until after the rockets are fired. Do you have any questions?"

Eric thought for a moment, then asked, "Why wouldn't all of the rockets fire?"

"Well," the officer answered, "Sometimes one of the rockets might get stuck in the launcher and the electrical contact won't connect; and sometimes there is a delayed action in the detonator. That is why it is so very important for you to get one of these unlaunched rockets overboard as quickly as possible before it explodes and damages the ship. This is a voluntary job and you don't have to take it if you don't feel that you can handle it."

"Oh No," Eric quickly countered. "I can do it just fine!"

The next couple of weeks were spent in intensive instruction on the Anti-Aircraft Guns, and by the time the ship was ready to sail to the South Pacific, everyone felt competent in their roles.

Chapter 2 - Eric on his Way to War

The first top on the way to 'War' was Pearl Harbor. LCSes only cruse at between 6 and 8 knots, so the trip took several days.

There were 12 other LCSes in the convoy, and although no one knew their destination, the scuttlebutt had it that they were getting ready to invade Japan itself. However, they were warned, there were a couple more islands that had to be taken first, and the closer they got to Japan, the harder the fighting would become.

When they reached Pearl Harbor, the crew, not on duty, stood silently at attention as they passed the ships that were destroyed on that 'Day of Infamy,' December 7, 1941.

"There are still sailors in the sunken hulls," he was told. This made Eric fiercely angry, he just couldn't wait to get into battle and avenge his fallen brothers.

After leaving Pearl Harbor, the task force of LCSes stopped at a couple of the small south sea Islands. At one, there wasn't a tree standing. The naval guns and aircraft had leveled everything. After taking the island, the Army had built a hasty supply base. There were several Quonset Huts, but most of the supplies were sitting in the open on pallets covered with canvas to shield them form the scorching sun.

The next stops were Guam and Saipan. These islands had not been fully secured and there were still Japanese forces holding out in the jungles. The harbors of the two islands were an interesting contrast. In Guam, the water was dark and murky. You couldn't see a foot below the surface. On the other hand, the harbor at Saipan was as clear as crystal. You could see the sandy bottom and the bottoms of the ships that had 10 and 12 foot drafts. At night you could see the phosphorous trails of the large fish feeding on the smaller fish.

Eric volunteered for the landing party that went ashore to help round up the Japanese troops that were still holding out in small pockets.

"Watch out for the Booby Traps!" they were warned. Attractive "souvenirs" were cleverly attached to explosives by the Japanese and placed for the unsuspecting GI to reach and retrieve the prize. When the prize was moved, it would cause an explosion that would destroy the prize, and the GI retrieving the prize. Eric's Party came across a couple of booby traps that they marked to caution others, but much to Eric's dismay they did not see any action against the Japanese forces.

When all of the landing parties got back to their ships, part of the task force was deployed to invade the Island of Iwo Jima, and the rest were instructed to get ready to invade the Island of Okinawa.

Iwo Jima turned out to be a bloody land battle; Okinawa was to become the biggest and most costly naval battle in history.

Chapter 3 - At Okinawa

Okinawa provided Eric with all of the action that he was looking for. The rocket launch on Tori Shima, one of the smaller islands in the Okinawa chain, went off in a spectacular blast, but one of the rockets lay unexploded in the launcher when Eric inspected after the firing.

"Get rid of it! Get rid of it!" the Captain shouted in panic.

"Aye, Aye, Sir," Eric responded.

Abounding in ignorance rather than raw courage, he quickly, but calmly went about his duty; retrieving the errant rocket and tossing it over the side. No sooner had the rocket hit the water than it exploded and sent up a torrent of sea water that drenched the side of the ship and all of the personnel in the vicinity, including Eric.

The Captain was noticeably shaken. "Why didn't you throw it up forward?" he shouted in a high pitched voice.

Eric made no response. He stood there puzzled for a moment, then quickly assembled his gun crew to get ready for any strafing airplanes. The landing was relatively easy. The island had heavy fortifications, but they were on the back edge of the beach. The rockets went up over the fortifications and exploded on the other side, destroying most of the forces that were waiting for the GIs to land and had no protection from the rear. The LCSes had delivered tons of explosives with their rockets and luckily they landed in just the right place.

"I wish that they had been this successful at Iwo Jima," one of the Officers commented. Rockets were a relatively recent innovation and had been used at Saipan, but it had taken some time before they reached the point where they could be used to their maximum efficiency. The task force commander had ordered the firing of the rockets at just the right time.

The next deployment took the task force to the harbor at the main Island where the big guns of the Battleships and Cruisers were bombarding the enemy installations. The noise of the big guns was deafening as the little ships entered the harbor, but when they got along side of the ships that were bombarding the Island, the noise turned to a dull thud.

Eric looked around and felt a bit disappointed, it looked like most of the exciting naval action was over and he had missed it. But the disappointment didn't last long. All of a sudden, literally hundreds of Japanese aircraft came swarming in from all sides. "Here come the Kamikazes." He was told.

The Kamikazes were the last ditch effort by the Japanese to protect their country from the approaching Allied Forces. These Kamikazes took an oath of suicide. They were Japanese pilots who aimed their explosive laden planes at allied naval vessels and at the forces invading the island, sacrificing their lives to destroy their targets. At Okinawa, there were also Kamikaze boats whose drivers took the same oath and had the same targets. These were small, high speed boats with explosives in the bow. The Japanese were loosing the war and they went all out to make Okinawa the largest and most costly Naval Battle on record. It was Eric's ship's job now to help defend against the Kamikazes. They were positioned around the large ships scanning both the air and the surface.

The LCSes were most effective against the 'skunks' as the suicide boats were called. Several of the skunks got through their fire power and some rammed the little gun boats when they realized that they couldn't get past the LCSes. Their drivers were dedicated to do as much damage as possible.

After several costly days and nights of intense attacks, the task force commander decided to take the offensive and scan the shore line to detect and blow up the skunks before they launched into the water. Eric's Captain was a recent U.S. Naval Academy graduate with no prior sea duty. He contacted another member of his graduating class on one of the big ships and requested to come along side for supplies. The two got to visiting and Eric's ship was well behind the rest of the task force as it headed out to scan the shore line. In an attempt to catch up with the others, the Captain ordered his ship to cut across a seemingly open area with out considering the fact that they were approaching low tide. The order was given, "All ahead at full speed."

Just as the ship was nearing the point that was closest to shore, there was a thunderous noise and the ship tilted to the side and stopped!

Was it a torpedo or a mine?

No, it was a coral reef!

"All engines back, flank speed!"

"Forward!" "Back!" "Forward!" "Back!"

The engines were burning up and all hands were sweating.

"It will be the middle of the night before high tide," a brilliant but snitty quartermaster reported. The two quartermasters on board were V-5 'washouts'

Short Stories and Tall Tales   57

and gave the impression that they were a cut above the rest of the crew. The snitty one was an accomplished musician and the other was a confident young man who thought that he knew more about seamanship than the Captain did; and he was probably right. 'Masters' as he was called by the crew, sailed on his family's yacht from the time he started to walk until the Navy confiscated it to use as a patrol craft along the Atlantic coast.

"Break out the small arms," the boatswain ordered. Eric and his gun crew were given the bow area to defend.

"Armed Japanese swimmers tried to board an LST a couple of nights ago and caused considerable damage, killing three sailors and wounding several others before they were destroyed," they were told.

Half-way through the mid-night watch, Eric saw a suspicious form floating toward the ship and radioed the conning tower. "Request permission to fire on suspicious form approaching at 10 degrees off starboard bow."

"Wait! Wait!" the excited Captain returned. "I don't want to give our position away unless I have to."

"Give our position away?" Eric mumbled. Here we are, 150 feet long and 50 feet high, sitting all by ourselves less than 100 yards from shore. . Who couldn't see us?

Just then the OOD came by and looked at the form. "It looks like a peach basket, but I think that there could be a swimmer pushing it. -- Eric, take a shot just behind that form and see what happens."

Eric took careful aim with a 30.06 Springfield and pulled the trigger. Something lunged behind the floating debris.

"It's a Jap swimmer!" the OOD shouted, "And he's headed for the ship."

Before the officer finished 'headed,' twenty sailors on the bow, the quarter deck and the starboard side of the main deck started firing. Three 50 caliber machine guns, eight automatic carbines, eight 30.06 rifles and a 20 MM Anti-Aircraft cannon wildly pounded a 200 square yard section of the water in the general vicinity of the swimmer. At least one of the shots hit the package that the 'swimmer' was pushing and a blinding explosion resulted.

All twenty sailors claimed credit for the kill. The claim was settled two months later when the Captain was officially credited with the destruction of an enemy mine and he was awarded the Bronze Star for heroism.

When high tide came, the ship floated free, and the 301 headed back to the harbor.

Chapter 4 - On the Picket Line

On the way back to the harbor, the word was received that the big ships had been hit by several surprise kamikaze air attacks the night before and had taken heavy casualties. The Admiral in charge had decided to take a bold action that would warn the ships when the Kamikazes were going to attack.

He ordered a task force of Destroyers and LCSes out into the ocean mid-way to Japan to detect oncoming waves of Japanese attackers and then radio back to the harbor to warn the big boys to get ready. This operation was known as the Okinawa Picket Line.

The destroyers with their state of the art radar at the time were deployed into sixteen designated locations. Each location, or station as they were called, had a destroyer with 5 or 6 LCS's to help defend them against the Kamikazes should they attack them out there.

The Picket Line was very successful and cut big ship casualties drastically. However, the Kamikazes soon switched their main targets from Okinawa and the big ships to the ships on the Picket line. The Picket Line casualties became horrendous. The destroyers, who were bigger and easier to hit, suffered the most but no one had an easy time.

All crews were at general quarters, ready to man the anti-aircraft guns around the clock. Those who weren't wounded were exhausted. Easter Sunday, April 1945, was the day that Eric made a promise to God that God forced him to keep before he got back to the States. He was at his battle station with his gun crew helping to defend the radar that was aboard the destroyer patrolling with them. The destroyer, with its sophisticated radar, cruised back and forth in the ocean between Japan and Okinawa, and a group of little gun boats (LCSes), including the 301, cruised on each side of the mighty ship to help ward off any Japanese suicide planes that would try to knock out the radar. That radar was the radar used to give warning to the American Forces fighting on Okinawa that the Jap Bombers were approaching.

It was during this time that the attacks were becoming much heavier on the picket line ships, and the crews were at general quarters about 90% of the time. Eric's ship was luckier than many of the other ships on the line. When their guns were firing, they seemed to be able to shoot down and ward off the attacking planes in their sector. However, for some reason lately, the guns would occasionally stop firing while fighting off the enemy. Fortunately, there were two other 40 MMs on Eric's ship and the ship managed to keep at least two guns going at all times.

There were two reasons for the gun stoppage; either a misfire or a short recoil. It was the gun captain's responsibility to determine what the problem was, and then to get the gun firing again.

There is a standard operating procedure to follow that takes between 30 and 60 seconds. The gun crew is ordered to leave the gun site immediately and the Gun Captain elevates the barrel, looking through the breech to see if there is a shell in the chamber. If there is, it is a misfire, and it is the Gun Captain's job to take out the shell and throw it overboard as quickly as possible before it explodes. If the barrel is empty, it is a short recoil and the Gun Captain simply pulls down a lever to cock the gun and the gun is ready for action.

If there is a misfire and the gun is re-cocked to fire again; the resuming of firing would explode the shell in the chamber as well as the second shell being fired. The result would be the destruction of the gun and gun crew as well as cause damage to the rest of the ship.

On this particular day, Eric's gun was firing at a Jap 'Betty' coming in off the bow. The other two 40's were firing at a plane coming in on the port side.

The destroyer was a little to the rear of the ship on the starboard side. Suddenly Eric's gun stopped. There wasn't time for the 30 to60 second standard procedure. Eric held the crew in their positions, prayed for a short recoil and cocked the gun,. He then gave the order to continue firing.

The pointer, who was an older, and more conservative than Eric looked at him with a most questioning stare. Eric again quickly shouted "Fire!," and the crew resumed firing to ward off the attacker.

When the planes had gone and no one was around, the pointer asked Eric, "How did you know that it was a short recoil?"

Eric replied, almost without thinking, "I saw the light." Even though it was at dusk with very little light, Eric was never questioned on this again.

At that time, honor and following orders were more important to Eric than life itself. He realized that failure to follow standard operating procedure was a serious offense and he also realized what could have happened if he had guessed wrong!

Short Stories and Tall Tales   61

There were many theories about what had happened that day. One of the crew members felt that when the gun stopped firing, the pilot momentarily lost sight of the ship and veered off to the side, Another crew member felt that the Betty, which was larger than most of the suicide planes, had an extra heavy bomb charge that was destined only for the destroyer and the radar aboard, and didn't want to waste it on the small LCS. The Pointer theorized that the pilot lost his nerve and changed his mind.

It was plain and simple to Eric, it was the hand of God that had saved them. Eric made a promise to God there and then, that he would publicly praise God for sparing them at the very first opportunity he had.

Eric had been raised in a Church where a time was set aside in each service for members to give a 'personal testimony' for any special blessings that they had received during the week. It had always been a cross for him to participate in this part of the service and he was totally embarrassed the one time his Grandmother forced him to do so. He made the promise to God that he would give a personal testimony and 'witness' for God the very first chance he got. This promise was soon forgotten as the ship continued duty on the picket line.

CHAPTER 5 - A QUIET DAY AT OKINAWA

Eric had just finished another tour on the 'Picket Line,' and his ship was back at the anchorage. It was an active tour and they had added another 'officially credited' jap plane on the Ship's conning tower. There wasn't nearly as much excitement and celebration this time as there was when they were credited for their first 'kill.' Many of the crew members were still teenagers who had grown a lot in the last two months, and with maturity, it seems, comes a certain quietness and reserve.

On their last day at the picket station they were cruising along on the port side of a two line formation in a quiet, uneventful fashion. Everyone was pretty tired as they had spent a good share of their time at general quarters the previous few days and the crew was looking forward to being back at the anchorage and sacking out.

It was cloudy and overcast as Eric and the others almost casually watched a streaking zero far off to the port side; apparently trying to avoid the Picket Station to get to Okinawa and hit one of the big ships. The Captain reported the plane and he was informed that the destroyer with them on the station had already alerted the forces back at the main base.

The Jap disappeared into the clouds and the ship returned to a dull quietness. All of the sudden, all hell broke loose! Off to the starboard, the Jap Zero was coming back in behind the two columns of LCS's and headed right for the rear of the destroyer. The 'five inchers' on the destroyer were pounding up shells in desperate rapidity while every gun on the LCSes in the back of the columns were sending hundreds of screaming tracers into the sky.

The LCSes in the front of the columns had to hold their fire as the ships were in a line where firing would have caused more damage to the ships than it would to the hated Jap.

Eric quickly looked around to see if there were other planes coming in, for this was not an uncommon maneuver for the Kamikaze to send in one plane to divert attention, then counter with two or three others. However, this was not a diversion. The Zero accomplished what looked like an impossibility, and exploded on the rear deck of the Destroyer.

When the smoke cleared, the rear end of the Destroyer was leveled to just above the water-line. The Five Inch Turret and everything that is usually on the afterdeck of a destroyer was no where to be found.

There was mass chaos aboard the stricken ship as the LCSes in the port column came along side to give assistance. Smoke was billowing from the stern section of the Destroyer and two sailors could be seen chasing a burning shipmate around the deck trying to stop him and put out the flames. In training, sailors are taught to roll on the ground or deck if their clothing catches on fire; but in the heat of the battle, sometimes panic overtakes the situation and greater disaster sets in.

"Fire Detail, prepare to board the ship," the Boatswain shouted.

Soon, Eric and seven other crew members dragged their hose aboard the Destroyer and headed for the smoke. One of the members of Eric's boarding party stumbled over the remains of a sailor who had been killed by the explosion.

"You're standing in the guy's stomach!" the Boatswain shouted.

Noticeably shaken, the sailor quickly pulled his foot away and went with the party to put out the fire. After the fire was under control, the shaken sailor began to cry uncontrollably. The Boatswain slapped him across the face several times but it was ineffective. Eric finally helped the devastated sailor back to the 301.

When the battered Destroyer was secured, one of the LCSes was designated to tow it to 'Wiseman's Cove, better known as the "Ship's Graveyard;" and the other LCSes were assigned to take on the Destroyer's crew members; burying the dead at sea, and transporting the wounded to a Hospital Ship.

But that was yesterday, and this morning, nearly everyone on the 301 was sleeping as Eric and two other crew members had the 'small boat duty.' They quietly waited for their watch to be over so they too could hit the sack.

Shortly into the watch, Eric got a call to pick up an injured sailor from another small ship and take the sailor to a larger ship that had a 'regular doctor' on board.

(The LCSes and small ships only had a pharmacist mate to take care of their health problems.)

When Eric's boat arrived at the LCM, two sailors were waiting on deck. One was deathly white and had a bloodied bandage at the end of his elbow where once an arm and a hand used to be. The other sailor was evidently the pharmacist mate; and neither said a word as they came on board.

Short Stories and Tall Tales 65

It was an awkwardly quiet trip to the big ship. The injured sailor passed out and the pharmacist mate quietly held him. It didn't seem like the time for small talk and they quietly delivered their passengers as quickly as possible.

Eric had no idea who either of the sailors were and never knew whether the injured man made it or not. It seemed cold and uncaring, but the Detail had completed their task and they quietly headed back to the 301.

Near the end of the watch, an order was given to pick up a floating body that was seen drifting near by. It was bloated and unrecognizable. Eric and the other sailors quietly fished the body out of the water and unceremoniously pushed it to the bottom of the boat. Even at the time it seemed as though something should be said, but what could be said? Normal feelings and curiosity were not a part of life that day. Duty and the completion of assigned tasks had become the only considerations. Their watch was nearly finished, and the remaining tasks were the duty of the next watch.

It wasn't long before Eric and his partners threw their tired bodies into their bunks and drifted into restless sleep. It was a quiet day, and it was a lousy day, but it was one of those days that Eric would never forget.

Chapter 6 - The Occupation

After a total of 82 days on the 'Picket Line' the Island of Okinawa was secured and the powers that be decided to end the operation and prepare for the final battle; the invasion of Japan itself.

Although the Japanese Air Force and Navy had been clearly defeated, there were still hundreds of thousands, and perhaps even millions of ground forces ready to defend their homeland to the death, just at the Kamikazes at Okinawa had vowed to do. It was expected to be the bloodiest invasion ever.

The LCSes were ordered to the Philippines to join up with the rest of the Invasion Force. Just before departing, a message was received for Eric. The Captain informed him that his Grandmother had died. Even though his Grandmother was his only close relative, Eric was not noticeably saddened by the news. He had a half of his pay sent to his Grandmother from the day he first enlisted, and he felt good about doing so. He had experienced death all around him for the last few months, and he had learned to accept it. Eric was alone, and actually he had been alone all of his life. He never seemed to form those bonds of friendship that many crew members form. He had had his fill of excitement and war, but he was eager to get into this last battle and avenge Pearl Harbor.

Just as the ships were ready to leave the Philippines for Japan, the news came through that the War in Europe had ended and that the U.S. had dropped a couple of A-Bombs on Japan. This had little effect on Eric; his war was in the Pacific and he really didn't know very much about an A-Bomb or the war in Europe.

His focus was on "The Last Battle," and when further news came through that Japan had surrendered, it was an emotional let down for him.

"Don't be fooled!" the Captain warned the crew. "These are the people that bombed Pearl Harbor while their Ambassador was talking peace with our President. They are also the people of the Kamikaze! Don't be surprised if they blow up their whole Island when we land as a final tribute to their Emperor."

The Invasion Force left for Japan, fully expecting another sneaky trick and the fulfillment of the promise of the bloodiest invasion ever.

The assignment of the LCSes was to dock at the Japanese Naval Base in Yokuska and the crews were to go on land to "test the waters."

When the ships arrived at Tokyo Bay, the crews were told that the Japanese were now a very friendly people, and that the crews would go into Tokyo and Yokohama on Liberty, "making a good impression on the people there."

Much to Eric's surprise, the crews did not encounter any hostility. The Japanese were very quiet and respectful, but he did not feel that they were the least bit friendly. Soon there seemed to be more soldiers and sailors on shore than there were Japanese. Eric was assigned Shore Patrol Duty and teamed up with the Military Police to keep law and order; not among the Japanese, but among the U. S. Military Forces on leave and liberty in the cities.

Less than two months previously, Eric and his crew had been on the "picket Line," with hatred in their hearts for the treacherous enemy, and now they were assigned to 'protect' these people from the sailors and soldiers that were their comrades in battle.

This seemed like a lot to expect from anyone, let alone a teenager. But these teenagers were not the regular teenagers. They had matured far beyond their years.

Shore Patrol became a bore, but Liberty after duty hours was interesting for a while. Eric was fascinated by the courageous little boys who came right up next to the war ships and fished to bring home supper for their families. He found himself sharing candy with some of them, and finally met a sister of one of the boys that spoke English.

Kim, as she was called, was a very attractive young lady! Her grandfather was a Russian Diplomat who married a Japanese woman and ran a small resort hotel at the foot of Mount Fujiyama. Their one daughter, Kim's mother, married an Air Force Pilot, Kim's father, who was killed in battle at Guam. Her older brother, only 19 at the time, was a Kamikaze Pilot killed at Okinawa.

Kim lived with her mother and younger brother on the outskirts of Yokohama, but when the occupation forces arrived, she was sent to stay with her grandparents. The Japanese expected the American Troops to rape and plunder as their troops had done in the Philippines and China; but when they discovered that this would not be the case, she came back to live in Yokohama.

The stories of Eric's kindness to her younger brother peeked Kim's interest, and she wanted to meet him.

Short Stories and Tall Tales 69

It was obvious that Eric was attracted to Kim from the very beginning. It had been quite some time since he had had any contact with the opposite sex, and he was vulnerable. When Eric found out that Kim's older brother had been a Kamikaze at Okinawa, he had mixed feelings. However, after they discussed it further, Eric not only understood her, he agreed with her completely.

"You were both men of honor and did what you had to do, "Kim explained. Her mother had been brought up in the Christian faith and she had passed on that faith to her daughter, but Kim's acceptance and forgiveness appeared much deeper than that of the Christians he had known back home.

Eric's faith was becoming much deeper also. He had gone from extreme hatred to understanding forgiveness in less than six months.

Kim's brothers embraced their father's religion, but much to Eric's surprise, the younger brother was just as understanding and forgiving as his sister. The mother was another matter.

"You are forbidden to speak with my daughter," Kim's mother told him. "There are many Geisha girls on the street for you," she shouted. When the fraternization between Kim and Eric continued, Kim was sent back to her grandfather's house.

Eric didn't see much of Kim's brother after that either, but one day, the brother saw him and told him how to find his grandfather's hotel. He then quickly stole away. Eric discovered that one could stay at a resort hotel for the weekend for scarce food items or cigarettes and he decided to try his luck at Kim's Grandfather's Hotel. Armed with a can of Vienna Sausage and a pair of woolen socks, he approached the grandfather for accommodations. He must have had the right combination, because he was immediately given a room with a sunken bath that was fed by the hot springs coming off Mt. Fujiyama. Eric later learned that he was expected and would probably have gotten a room no matter what he had brought.

The Grandfather asked Eric to come into his office, and after several probing questions, Kim was summoned in to meet with them. It was determined that Eric would be a good choice for a husband for Kim, and with the grandparent's encouragement and cooperation, their relationship blossomed.

When orders came through for Eric's ship and crew to return to the States, Eric approached his Captain with the request that he be allowed to stay on duty in Japan.

The Captain roared with laughter, "Got yourself stuck on a little Geisha girl, eh" he chuckled.

"No Sir, this is not a Geisha girl, and I intend to marry her," Eric protested.

"We sail tomorrow morning," the Captain said sternly, "And you either be on board ready to sail or you'll spend the rest of your time in the Brig!"

Eric was not able to make contact with Kim or anyone who could get a message to her; and the next morning, he was on board ready to sail.

CHAPTER 7 - THE JOURNEY HOME

It was the middle of the Monsoon Season when the ships left port, but no one seemed concerned. The entire crew, with the exception of Eric, was elated over the fact that they were going home.

"I'm going to join the 52/20 Club when I get back," one of the sailors happily shouted.

"What's the 52/20 Club?" Eric asked.

"We're all entitled to an unemployment check of $20.00 a week for a full year," came the answer.

"Not me!" snapped the snitty quartermaster. "I'm going to use the G.I. Bill to finish college."

"What's the G.I. Bill?" the bewildered Eric exclaimed.

The snitty quartermaster was quick to respond, "If you didn't spend so much time with your Geisha girl you'd know that every veteran is entitled to one year of college for every year spent in the service. The Government pays for all of the college costs and gives you $65 a month to live on."

Eric was about to let everyone know that Kim was not a Geisha girl but he was so depressed that he didn't feel like expending the energy.

On the second day at sea, they started to run into rough water. The scuttlebutt was passed around that a monsoon was headed their way. Eric had been in storms at sea before, but he never experienced anything like this monsoon. Waves reached the height of 80 feet and the 301 was tossed about like a volley ball. The bow of the 301 would sink under the water completely covering his antiaircraft gun and the rocket launchers; then, slowly rise up and extend 20 to 30 feet out of the water, only to slam down and again disappear.

"Head into the wind!" the Captain shouted. Only once did the 301 get caught side wind, but once could have been the end. The ship almost capsized to the starboard, but miraculously it headed back into the wind and stayed afloat. A number of men kept a constant prayer vigil in the mess hall, while one was seen raising his fist cursing God.

For the first time, Eric was concerned for his life. He thought about his experience at Okinawa and he thought about his Grandmother and the people back home. The one thought that kept coming back to haunt him was the promise he had made to God when his gun stopped firing on the Picket Line. He tried to console himself that he had never had a chance to publicly thank God since that time; but was it that he didn't have a chance, or that he never thought to keep his promise?

The fierce storm left as quickly as it came, but the huge swells continued for another two days. At the top of the swell you could see the entire convoy, some ships at the top of the swells and some at the bottom. Then, at the bottom of the swell there was nothing to see but water.

A little over three weeks after leaving Tokyo Bay, the convoy staggered into Pearl Harbor for refueling before continuing on to the States. Eric went on short liberty into Honolulu without a thought on his mind other than getting back home. Suddenly, he heard a Salvation Army Band in the distance. Immediately, he felt God's presence. It was not a beautiful feeling as you might think, it was a very depressing feeling. It was depressing because God was reminding him of his promise, and it was a promise that he did not relish keeping.

Eric's heart was pounding as he followed the Band to the Salvation Army Citadel and he went in and sat down for the service. When the testimony period came, his heart was pounding and his mouth was so dry that his lips stuck together. There was a short pause after the last testimony and Eric started to get up, but he was physically weak and almost fainted. Eric thought of every excuse under the sun and 'promised' that he would witness just as soon as he got back to the States.

Eric hurried back to his ship, but as he arrived, the ship was pulling out and his sea bag with transfer orders to another ship was sitting on the dock. He knew that God had punished him, but he did not know at the time that this was not the end of his punishment.

The ship that Eric was transferred to was an old LCI that was being overhauled to take the trip back to the States. It was scheduled to leave in three days, but when the departure time came, one of the engines failed and the trip had to be rescheduled for the following week. Eric was beginning to feel sorry for himself and felt that God was being unfairly hard on him. He had promised to witness just as soon as he got back to the States, and he stubbornly stayed on the ship while other crew members went on liberty, until finally, they set sail with several other LCIs.

Short Stories and Tall Tales　　73

Near the end of the first day out to sea, Eric's ship sprung a leak on the starboard side and began to take on water. The ship was ordered to return to Pearl Harbor, and about half way back, the engines gave out and the ship was without electrical power. It was dark, the ocean was getting rough and the ship was listing badly. If you have ever been out on that big ocean in a little ship that is sinking with nothing or no one in sight, you may have an idea of how Eric felt. He thought of the Biblical story of Jonah and the Whale, and how Jonah ended up in the belly of a whale because he refused God's command to go to Nineveh and witness for the Lord. Eric was convinced that he was about to enter the depths of hell. He doubted very much that a whale would come along and spit him up safely on land.

Eric frantically looked through the Gideon Testament that was given to him by God's servants at his induction into the Navy. He had read it from cover to cover once, but had read Matthew many times. Matthew had everything, he felt; the life of Christ, the miracles, the sermon on the mount; everything, including the passage he was looking for now. It was one that he had read many times, and one that was weighing heavily on him at this time.

Eric's hand trembled. "There it is - IF ANY MAN DENY ME BEFORE MEN HERE ON EARTH, I WILL DENY HIM BEFORE THE FATHER IN HEAVEN"

Eric had refused to witness as he had promised. He had denied Christ before men here on earth; now Christ would deny knowing him on Judgment Day!

This was not just a simple case of a sailor facing the end of his earthly life; he had faced that many times before. This was the case of a soul facing damnation in Hell for ever and ever.

Eric pleaded for just one more chance. But he had had one more chance may times. There comes a time when there are no more chances left.

With God's help, the ship finally made it back to Pearl Harbor, and it was condemned to the junk pile. Eric could hardly wait for Sunday to get back to the Salvation Army Citadel. His heart was pounding and his mouth was dry, but he was the first one on his feet at the testimony session. He had no idea what he said. He didn't remember a word; but it must have satisfied God for he was on another ship that week and made it back to the States without further incident. Eric had learned that when you make a promise to Almighty God to do something, you had better do it as soon as possible.

THE JEWISH YANKEE

The Jewish Yankee in Nazi Germany

CHAPTER I

Solomen Swartz was the son of Helwig Swartz, a Jewish emigrant from Germany who came to America shortly after WWI. The elder Swartz was fluent in the German language as well as English and he made his living, meager as it was, translating German college text books into English for the graduate education programs at several New York City Universities.

Helwig taught his son to speak German and often told him stories about his homeland over the objections of his Irish bride, Mary Theresa Kelley. The Germany that Helwig came from was orderly and neat. Even the forest floors were cleared and as a young boy he played among the trees. It was a happy time for Helwig, but he longed for the great opportunities that America offered, and he joined the many immigrants at that time in the quest for the 'pot of gold.'

Helwig did not find a 'pot of gold,' but he did become a true American and married a pretty little Irish girl. Life was not always rosy but they did their best to raise their only child, Solomen.

Unfortunately, Solomen had a troubled youth. He was not accepted by the Jewish community because his mother was Irish; and he wasn't accepted by the Irish community that he lived in, because his father was Jewish. He didn't like being half and half but his father was a very wise man who taught him to be tolerant and to be independent and self-reliant.

When Solomen graduated from high school, he decided not to go on to college even though his father had scrimped and saved enough for him to do so. Instead, Solomen took his inheritance and traveled to Germany. He was intrigued by the many stories that his father had told him and he felt that he might find the acceptance in Germany that he had failed to find in America.

When Solomen arrived in Germany, he soon discovered that there was a hatred toward the Jewish people in that Country and that a politician named Hitler made it a great honor to be a German. He had had enough of 'half and half' already, and he decided to become a member of the privileged race for a change. He stayed clear of the Jewish community and found enthusiastic acceptance as a German from America; especially from the frenzied followers of Hitler. He didn't exactly know what the Nazis stood for but he was used to one group of people discriminating against another group, so as long as he had the safety of being in a group that he could be supported by, it didn't seem to matter what they stood for.

Solomen joined the Nazi Party because it was the thing to do. After a while he discovered that it was the only thing to do, and stay alive. When the Nazi Party openly started to kill Jews and send them to concentration camps, Solomen was incensed. Discrimination is one thing, but killing is another, he reasoned. Solomen tried to escape, but he was trapped. To openly oppose the party would be suicide, and so he became half and half once again. One half was the Nazi Party member that was his front to society; the other half was an American that did everything he could in secret to help the Jewish victims. He just knew that there had to be others in the country who were against this vile action, but try as he would, he could not locate a one.

It was dangerous to even try to find a fellow sympathizer, but it was even more dangerous to help Jewish people in need. Many times Solomen thought that his end had come. He was in the communication division of the Nazi party and had access to information such as where and when the Gestapo Troops were going to raid a Jewish community.. As often as he could, he sneaked a warning to the people to flee the impending doom. Some ignored the warning, some just couldn't do anything about it, but some escaped; and somehow that was justification for his existence.

CHAPTER II

One day Solomen met a Jewish leader referred to as "Mo" that he felt he could trust. Solomen stole 26 Nazi youth uniforms and a Youth leader's uniform and smuggled them to Mo. The ingenious Mo dressed himself and the 26 young boys in the uniforms and marched them through the streets, on to a train, then on to a bus, and finally over the border to Switzerland. Mo them came back and organized an underground trail out of Germany.. Solomen felt that at last he had found a real purpose for his life.

Solomen and Mo hadn't arranged more than a dozen escapes before the German authorities sensed that there was a "leak" in their ranks. Solomen halted his activities for a while to protect his identity, but the frustrated officer in charge of his unit, unable to determine where the leak was, ordered the entire staff to different locations. Solomen was ordered to a concentration camp for duty. This was the most horrible duty that he could possibly get.

Solomen's assignment at the concentration camp was as a guard of the gas chamber. He had only briefly heard about the gas chambers and wasn't quite sure that what he had heard was true. However, when he saw the prisoners lined up to enter the chambers, he realized that the unbelievable stories that he had heard were indeed true. He was frantic. He couldn't possibly be a party to this action, and he couldn't possibly stop it. In a desperate move, he loosened a connection in the pipe line near where the Commanding Officer and his staff were to stand and observe the proceedings. After the prisoners were led into the chamber and the Commanding Officer and his staff were summoned to their positions, the order was given to feed the gas into the chamber.

Almost immediately, the gas shot out toward the Nazi Officers. Shouts and yells filled the air. The choking Commander ordered, "Achtung, Achtung!" The killings were postponed, at least for a few days, but Solomen questioned if he had really caused more harm than good. Most of the prisoners were skin and bone and seemed like they were dead already; but he did notice a sly grin on a couple of the prisoner's faces when they found out what had happened to the Nazi Officers. This was some gratification for his action. but now, he was on the hot seat again. The investigation came close to putting the blame on him, but miraculously he was cleared. Too soon, the chambers were ready again and the prisoners were back facing extinction. Solomen was absolutely helpless this time, and then the gas was started he passed out. When Solomen awoke, he was on his way to the medical unit. He convinced the technician in charge that he was allergic to the gas and he was transferred to another assignment. This transfer led to one of the most incredible stories to come out of World War II!

Solomen's new assignment was at a large estate in the suburbs of Hamburg. He was on the staff to guard 14 young Jewish girls and an older, but extremely attractive, Jewish woman. The girls were specially selected for their intelligence and beauty, and were to bear children for high ranking German officers who were single or whose wives were barren. The older woman, named Sylvia, was opposed to this and did what she could within her limited power to sabotage the operation.

Solomen learned through the other guards that Sylvia was the Head of an exclusive girl's school, and that she had agreed to cooperate in an effort to save the girls from the gas chamber. She did everything possible to stall for time with the hope that some miracle would happen. Little did Solomen know that he would become that miracle, and little did he know the bizarre way in which the miracle would take place.

Solomen found out that Sylvia was to send the girls individually to the officers during their fertile periods, but she waited for the menstrual period for each one and sent them for duty.

The officers complained but Sylvia said, "You asked for virgins and of course this is to be expected. "But," several of the officers said, "We never touched them!" The trauma alone is enough to break the delicate membranes, "Sylvia explained. The gullible officers accepted this foolish explanation and waited for Sylvia to send the girls in again at the right time. This was a great strategy, but of course, it could only be used one time for each of the girls.

Another delaying action strategy was a 'virus' that Sylvia said might give the officers Herpes unless they waited until the virus was arrested. By the time that Solomen came along, Sylvia had just about run out of strategies. Solomen secretly introduced himself to Sylvia and offered to help. Sylvia cautiously checked him out with some connections she had established and then put her trust in Solomen.

The Commanding officer's patience was just about at its end. They had determined the fertile periods for each of the girls and the ranking officer ordered Sylvia to produce his girl without further delay. Sylvia and the girls

Short Stories and Tall Tales

were devastated, and she asked Solomen if there was anything that he could do. Solomen promised that he would do his best. He got hold of some salt peter and sneaked a dose of it into the officers food that was enough to neuter a horse for a month.

The officers were greatly embarrassed, but the girls were spared another month. Solomen's plan worked so well that he sneaked into the kitchen and continued to saturate the officer's food with the impotent little miracle. It was several months before the supply of salt peter was exhausted and the officer in charge again ordered 'the program' to begin without any further delay or he would send the entire group, including Sylvia, to the gas chambers.

Sylvia was devastated and again begged for Solomen's help. Solomen told her that there was absolutely nothing else that he could do. "Oh yes you can," Sylvia said. "You will have to impregnate each of the girls before they go to the officers. I will not allow these girls to bear a Nazi child. You are a true Jew and you owe this to your people."

Solomen put up a mild protest, but he did not think that it was the proper time to announce that his mother was Irish. "But," stammered Solomen, "I have no experience! "Solomen had never let himself get close to anyone for fear of exposing the double identity that he had maintained most of his life. He had never been with a woman.

Sylvia smiled, "I will teach you all that you need to know!"

Sylvia did in deed teach Solomen all that he needed to know, and then some. He imagined that he had died and gone to heaven. Solomen performed his duty with relish and distinction, but Sylvia was by far his most cherished experience.

When the Nazi's were satisfied that all of the girls were pregnant, they were left alone under guard. Solomen and Sylvia continued a close fraternization, and as one might expect, Sylvia became pregnant as well.

Chapter III

Solomen's personal paradise soon came to an end. The Allies had invaded and Germany was on the brink of defeat. The order came through for Solomen and all of the other able bodied men to go to the front lines in a last desperate attempt to stop the enemy advance.

"You're not going," Sylvia said. "Get me a Nazi Uniform and get this message to Schultz. "Sylvia explained to him that when Germany surrendered, he would be a prisoner of war, and even though he was innocent, he would have an extremely hard time proving it. "They will all have some kind of story," she said, "And I'm afraid that they will have a great laugh at yours."

Solomen was surprised that Schultz was someone that would help. He had known him as a quiet Nazi Official that kept to himself. Solomen feared him and kept away from him as much as possible. "There are quite a few sympathizers in the Nazi ranks who do what they can but they must be extremely careful of being caught, "Sylvia told him.

"But why don't they band together and oppose these horrible crimes?" Solomen questioned.

"Some tried," Sylvia said, "But they are either dead or in concentration camps themselves. What they are doing is the most helpful role that they can play."

In less than two hours, Sylvia had a small Army bus and with the help of some forged papers that she had secured; Solomen, Sylvia and the 14 girls were headed for the Swiss border.

Sylvia explained to the Captain of the Guard that the girls were an embarrassment to some of the high ranking Nazi Officers and that she was ordered to take the girls to Switzerland until a treaty was signed. Solomen was the guard to see that she carried our her orders.

There was little trouble getting through the German border, and Mo was there waiting for them on the Swiss side. Solomen was greeted as a hero, but his glory time was short lived.

The Jewish religious leaders were not pleased with Solomen's exploits. The children will all have Jewish mothers and consequently they will be Jewish. But, Solomen was not a Jew, he had an Irish mother.

"How did they know?" Mo had told of Solomen's help when he first marched the young group of boys to freedom. Jewish Intelligence was, and probably always will be, among the best in the world, and they knew everything about Solomen before he arrived—except his extra ordinary service with Sylvia's girls.

When Sylvia heard about Solomen's heritage, she felt betrayed as well. She emotionally agreed that the best thing for all concerned was for Solomen to go back to America and forget what he had done in Germany the past 20 years.

"I feel like I have dug up a fortune, and now I have to bury it," the dejected Solomen lamented.

"Perhaps it is better to walk away without the fortune than to walk away with it and get shot in the back of the head," Sylvia countered.

The next morning Solomen went to the Airport to get a plane for New York City. Just before he boarded the plane he heard a voice call, "Solomen." he knew right away that it was Sylvia's voice. He turned and saw the most beautiful, radiant Sylvia. Pregnancy does this to a women sometimes.

"You are the fortune that I will really miss," Solomen told her, then he turned sadly away and continued on to the plane.

"Solomen!" the voice sounded once more. Again Solomen turned.

"Perhaps I'll see you some day in New York," she said.

The corners of Solomen's mouth started to turn up and a smile broke out. "See you in New York!" he replied.

The Jewish Yankee In The Promised Land

CHAPTER I

The Captain announced over the speaker system that the plane was starting its descent for landing. It had been a long trip. The lady who sat next to Solomen had talked non-stop the entire journey. Solomen felt that he knew all three of her former husbands intimately; and of course, he knew that she was currently unattached, for she had told him this close to a hundred times during the conversation.

The conversation? Actually there was little conversation. It was a case of the lady talking and Solomen listening. His experience in life had made him a very private person and he knew all of the strategies to avoid answering personal questions. In fact, his fellow passenger didn't even know his name until there were about to part upon leaving the plane when she point blank asked, "Gracious me, I don't even know your name. What is your name?"

"Solomen Swartz," he answered.

"And where are you from?"

"I was born right here in New York City; have a good day!"

Solomen melted into the crowd and was out of sight before another word could be uttered. It had been a little over twenty years since he had been in New York. My, how things had changed; and yet, so much was just the same. The apartment house he used to live in was still there but he didn't find anyone he knew, and no one seemed to have any idea of who Helwig and Mary Swartz were. Finally Solomen came across an elderly gentleman on the street that he did not remember; but the old fellow remembered Helwig Swartz's son.

"I believe that your father is working in the Air Plane Factory on Long Island, and your mother has moved up to an Irish settlement in the Catskills," the old man told him.

"My mother is not with my father?" Solomen questioned with an obvious pained expression. "She left almost twenty years ago, and your father left a year or two after that!"

Solomen hadn't corresponded with his parents in the over twenty years he had been away with the exception of a couple of short notes he had sent shortly after arriving in Germany.

Solomen had many pressing problems on his mind. When would he see Sylvia again, if ever? What was he going to do with his life back in America? Would his past come back to haunt him? However, none of these problems were more pressing at the moment than the desire to see his father again.

"I'm looking for Helwig Swartz! "Solomen must have said this a hundred times. Finally he was told, "Helwig works the afternoon shift and he lives in Flushing. "The receptionist wrote down the address and Solomen was on his way.

When Helwig saw his son, he cried. It had been so long. He had just about reconciled himself to the fact that Solomen had been killed in the War, but here he was, alive and well. There was so much to tell each other. Solomen's story was vague and without detail; but his father did not press him. It didn't matter to him what Solomen did; he knew that he did the best he could. The only thing that mattered was that he was well, and he was here with him

On the other hand, Solomen wanted to know everything. What happened to his Mother? Who is the woman that his father is living with now? Did his father and mother ever see each other?

It seemed that after Solomen had left, Helwig and his mother had little in common. They went on a vacation to East Durham, an Irish community in the Catskills, and his mother decided to stay there. Helwig went to work in a defense factory on Long Island and met a Christian Jewish woman who made him feel that life was worth living. She ultimately became his wife.

Helwig was a philosophical man and was not enamored with the political part of Judaism, but he dearly loved much of his Jewish tradition. His new wife Sarah basically felt the same, but she also embraced Christianity as the fulfillment of Jewish prophesy. Sarah also embraced Solomen into their home, and it was decided that Solomen would move in with them until he established a home of his own.

"Maybe I can get a job at your plant," Solomen suggested.

"Not on your life," his father snapped back. "You are far too bright to waste your time in a factory. You are going back to college.The place for you is on Wall Street.

Chapter II

Solomen settled on a two year program in accounting at NYU. He found business fascinating. Solomen's enthusiasm stimulated Helwig's thinking and He decided to buy into a small partnership of a garment factory on the lower east side of New York City.

After Solomen's first term at NYU, he spent his spare time in his father's factory helping the bookkeeper and learning about the garment industry. When Solomon graduated with his Associates Degree, he got a job with an investment firm on Wall Street; but he still spent his spare time at the garment factory.

"You should incorporate and expand," Solomen told his father. "We're working full time now!" Helwig responded, "And we have all of the money we need."

"Father," Solomen continued in a calm but desperate attempt to explain the seriousness of his argument. "American Economy is changing. You can't just stand still, you must go dramatically forward or you will go bust-up backward. The whole idea is to produce more and more and make greater and greater profit."

"I took advantage of the benefit of free classes for employees when I worked at the college, and I learned a bit about economics too," Helwig protested. "There's a thing called the Business Cycle that is as basic as the principle of supply and demand. We have a boom now, but if we over-produce, the supply will become greater than the demand and we will go into recession. Those who have expanded too much will go 'belly-up" when the depression hits."

"Father, Father, Father. The new government policy eliminates depression. That is why the thrust is to produce more and more. The Players, that is the bankers, the businessmen and politicians who run the system, have it all figured out. When things start to slow down, the government will step in, regulating interest rates; subsidizing business enterprises to expand; and even giving money to the large corporations that would put thousands of workers on unemployment and hurt the overall economy if they were to fold up."

'So, there will be some losers in this policy of prosperity," Helwig interjected.

"Of course there will be some losers," Solomen snapped back. "The players know this, and they have enacted laws to allow the players to start over again. That's the whole idea of the corporation. The CEO, the head of the corporation, takes his chances on big profits with other people's money. If he makes a poor decision and goes bankrupt, and the government laws can't help him, his personal wealth is protected and he can start over again in another corporation."

"What about the poor people who invested their money in theCorporation?" Helwig questioned.

"Most of that money will come from investors, government grants, etc. Some investors will win and some will loose. It is planned that there will be a great body of investors, including foreign investment, that will keep the system going. The hope of winning will be the key."

Solomen paused for a minute and then continued. "There will be some people that will be hit hard, middle management and the workers; -- and there may be a lot of rebellion and crime among the unfortunate. There may even be small wars around the world; but those who know what they are doing and play the game will make out just fine.

"I'll bet that the taxes will go sky high," Helwig added.

"But of course," Solomen answered with a matter of fact gesture, "But that won't hurt the players. There will be loop holes and they will have more than enough surplus to take care of any tax increase.

"Both men remained uncomfortably quiet for a brief time, and then, Solomen tried to brighten things up. "There is an up side too! There will be billionaires instead of millionaires. The average worker will make more money in a day than they do in a week now. Just about everyone will have a car and many other luxuries that we haven't even dreamed about yet."

"Will they be happier in this new system?" Helwig asked.

"Probably not," Solomen responded candidly. "The motivating factor for everyone is to be a 'top winner;' and of course, only a few can be at the top. The whole philosophy is to keep climbing. No one will have time to be happy as we think of happiness now!"

"What a strange philosophy," Helwig muttered. "It's getting late. Let's talk about this another time."

The next time Solomen and Helwig got together for a serious conversation, Helwig started the ball rolling with, "I've given your thoughts a lot of

Short Stories and Tall Tales   89

consideration, and I agree with the contention that we must go forward to keep up with the pace, but I still like owning and operating my business without trying to exploit other people's savings. I've decided to set up two shifts at the factory. The money saved in capital expansion can be shared with the workers in higher wages."

Solomen could not fault his father's thinking. It was morally appealing to his inner feelings, but it would not give Helwig the maximum return for his business.

"And what will you do after expanding to two shifts, go on to three shifts? You can't go beyond three shifts, you know!"

Helwig expected some flack from Solomen but he had made up his mind what he was going to do. "We'll take care of that when the time comes," he said.

Solomen just smiled. He was establishing his own Mutual Fund Operation with 'other people's money' and he would just wait and see who made out the best.

CHAPTER III

Solomen's knowledge of the Stock Market paid off big. He was close to being a millionaire in his first year and was a multi-millionaire three years later. He made many friends, but he also made a few enemies too. The wife of one of his business associates came into his office one day with a gun and attempted to hill him, but he fortunately escaped with only a minor wound. A minor physical wound, that is. Solomen liked his Associate, but business is business. The Associate made a poor business decision and he had to suffer the consequences. The distraught fellow did not play the game and start over again. Instead, he took his own life in a tragic suicide. Solomen gave generously to the widow to help her out, but deep inside he could not justify his business actions in this case. Everything he did was perfectly legal to be sure, but was he morally right? Helwig never discussed his business with him, but he knew that Helwig was not pleased with the way he handled his business affairs . Solomen was ruthless in business, but so were almost all of the business people that he dealt with. He did what he had to do to succeed. Helwig, on the other hand, was not quite as successful, although he did well and did expand to a new, bigger factory. His factory was one of the very few that did not have a union, and consequently never went on strike.

Helwig had a profit sharing arrangement with his workers that both he and his workers thought was fair. Solomen had told him many times that he was far too generous, but it was obvious that Helwig enjoyed a much happier business experience than did Solomen. Helwig took his whole work staff for a two week winter vacation to Florida every year. It wasn't at the most expensive resort in Florida but it was adequate and he struck a deal for the whole Hotel.

Everyone seemed to have a great time. Solomen tried to explain to his father that the objective for incentive programs was to get increased production from employees, but Helwig maintained that his employee benefits were gifts for loyalty and service.

Solomen visited several times during the vacation periods and had to admit that he never heard a complaint from anyone. Sarah was also on all of the factory vacations and spent quite a bit of time in the factory as well.

Solomen had grown quite fond of Sarah. He could see that she and Helwig had a very special relationship that he wished he could have had with Sylvia. He was beginning to think more and more about Sylvia, and finally decided he to take matters into his own hands. Like his father had warned him, he was so busy making money that he forgot about having a good time.

CHAPTER IV

The excursion to Israel was going to cost quite a bit of money, but money wasn't a problem with Solomen. Solomen found out that Sylvia was living in a settlement with his daughter, almost 10 years old now.

Why hadn't Sylvia come to New York as she had promised? He had wasted ten years waiting for her, he thought. But really, was he waiting? No, the truth was that Solomen was busy making money. He had decided not to waste any more time so he got on a plane destined for Israel..

When Solomen saw Sylvia, she looked much older and she reflected hard work and sadness. Sylvia wasn't in Israel long when it was revealed that she too was not a true Jew. Her mother was German, and one of the first to protest the unfair treatment of the Jews by the Third Reich; and she was one of the first to be sent to the detention camps, never to return. This did not count much in the pecking order of the New Israel, and Sylvia found herself and her daughter outside the select circle. She just never seemed to get the better opportunities. In addition, she was in great disfavor for her actions with the young girls that had been put in her charge, and the powers that be never understood or forgave her for this.

"Why didn't you come to New York?" Solomen asked.

Sylvia look at him as if she could not believe the question.

"How," she answered. "Do you think I have wings to fly?"

Solomen took her into his arms. Both were soon in tears as Solomen promised to take them back to America with him. Sylvia told him that this would be impossible. Sylvia was almost right, it was near impossible for Sylvia to leave with him. Rachael, the daughter he had never seen before, had difficulty getting out of the country; and Sylvia definitely would not leave without her. Solomen proved the old adage, 'Money Talks,' and he now had a very loud voice.

Rachel was the beauty that Solomen knew Sylvia was when she was an adolescent. It took a little while, but he finally convinced Rachael that he too had problems being accepted when he was growing up; but he had solved these problems in America and he would help her to solve them there too. When they flew over the Statute of Liberty, Solomen assured Sylvia and Rachael that this was the Promised Land for the three of them.

When Solomen, Sylvia and Rachael united again with Helwig and Sarah, he was shocked with the startling news that Sarah was expecting. Sarah was considerably younger than Helwig, and Solomen had a difficult time accepting the situation. He was going to have a sibling almost fifty years younger than he! Incredible!

"Well, at least he or she won't be half and half," Solomen blurted out. Solomen always felt that something was missing in his life and that he was not a 'total' person. Helwig sensed this and tried to console him."Solomen, we are what we are. When Sylvia and Rachael get their citizenship's, we will all be true Americans, and that's about the best you can get in this life," Helwig philosophized.

"You don't understand," Solomen protested. "You were a true Jew and you had no idea how it was to be half and half!"

Helwig looked thoughtfully away from Solomen, then turned back.

"Solomen," he said, "My mother's mother was Polish.'

Solomen was silent, as was everyone else in the room. Then Solomen started to smile. He was quickly joined by the others, and soon endorphins filled the room. Finally being half and half didn't matter. They were Americans and they could be true Americans, being themselves.

God had blessed America more than any other nation in the world. They were among the luckiest people on earth.

THE VOLUPTUOUS CORPS

AT THE CEMETERY

"What a waste!"

"She was the most beautiful woman I have ever seen. Why did this happen?"

There were just a handful of people at the grave site on that hot, overcast day. "She's even had more husbands than this," one of the observers said in a half serious smirk.

It was true, Holly Malloy had many close, intimate relationships in her lifetime; almost all with the opposite sex. The one exception was the lone woman standing by her grave site, Mag Horrihan. Mag wasn't the last of Holly's lovers, but she was the only one that came to her funeral.

Holly was head cheerleader, homecoming queen, prom queen for both the Junior and Senior Class; and definitely the most idolized person to ever graduate from Lexington High. When she walked, it was as if the most talented and beautiful ballerina was giving her greatest performance. She was jokingly referred to as a three letter 'jock', although she never played any sports. Holly was the girl friend of the captain of the football team during football season, the 'steady' of the captain of the basketball team during basketball season, and the 'lover' of the captain of the baseball team during baseball season. Her quest for new and better lovers didn't end with high school graduation. She was always looking for higher mountains to climb right up to the end; and the mountains were always ready to obey her slightest request.

"Whoever put that nylon cord around her neck and pushed her off the deck must have really hated her. The thin line cut through the juggler vein and produced one of the bloodiest messes I have ever seen!" Detective Morelli exclaimed.

Pat Morelli had been a homicide detective for almost 30 years and had seen a great many 'bloody messes. His companion, Father Broadhurst, had been closer to the Malloy family than anyone in the town. The good Father had a very special concern for Holly. He had always maintained that Holly was an unhappy, confused soul; and not the ambitious, ruthless manipulator that everyone else thought her to be.

"I've got to look over her apartment for anything my partner may have missed," said Detective Morelli. "Want to come along Father?" Father Broadhurst willingly went along.

AT THE APARTMENT

"Will you look at this, the Holy Bible. That's the last thing I would have expected to see in Holly Malloy's apartment," mumbled the aging detective.

"I'm not the least bit surprised," said the Priest. "She was always number one in her catechism class."

Father Broadhurst picked up the Bible and started to leaf through it. "Mmm, that's strange. This verse is highlighted. 'It is easier for a camel to go through the eye of a needle than it is for a rich man to enter the kingdom of heaven.'"

"That's not much help," grunted Morelli. "Every man she ever went out with was rich. What I need to know is which rich man hated her, or loved her so much, that he had to do her in."

"For a detective," retorted the Priest, "You know very little about human nature. First of all, you are one hundred percent wrong in your assessment of Holly Malloy; and as for murder because of love, no murder was ever committed because of love."

"What about the husband who pulled the plug on his wife who was suffering with cancer?" snapped the detective trying to get one up on his adversary.

The Priest completely ignored Morelli and went on leafing through the pages. "What's this? It's in Holly's hand writing!"

"Let me see it," shouted the excited detective as he grabbed the small piece of paper. It's easier for a camel to go through the eye of the needle than it is for a beautiful woman to enter into the state of happiness. That doesn't make any sense at all!"

"I'm afraid it makes all kinds of sense," Father Broadhurst said in a sad, slow response. "It tells me that this was a very sad and disillusioned young lady that may have taken her own life. The Holly I know," he continued, "Did not provoke hatred, she inspired love. Two of the husbands that I knew personally actually accepted their separation from Holly with a genuine appreciation for the time that had spent with her and would welcome her back if she ever cared to do so."

Short Stories and Tall Tales

"That's a weird thesis, Father. You need more than intuition to make a decision in my business!"

"Take a look at this! Maybe this will convince you." Father Broadhurst handed Morelli a short poem written in Holly's own handwriting. "This was not copied, it was written from the heart. "Detective Morelli read aloud, "DISILLUSIONED!"

> YOU START YOUR LIFE ALL STARRY EYED AND DREAM OF A PERFECT END.
>
> RIGHT IS RIGHT AND WRONG IS WRONG, ON THAT YOU CAN DEPEND.
>
> YOU BEGIN THE LONG HARD JOURNEY THAT LEADS YOU TO SUCCESS,
>
> YOUR GOALS ARE ALL THOSE PRECIOUS THINGS THAT OTHER FOLKS POSSESS.
>
> SOON YOU FIND THAT SUCCESS IS BUILT ON THINGS NOT ALWAYS RIGHT;
>
> YOU CHANGE YOUR GOALS, YOUR DREAMS, YOUR WAYS AND ENTER IN THE FIGHT.
>
> WHEN AT LAST YOU REACH THE TOP AND VIEW THE THINGS YOU'VE WON,
>
> A SAD SICK FEELING FILLS YOUR SOUL, FOR THE GAINS YOU WANT ARE NONE.

"You theorize that the beautiful Holly was disillusioned and took her own life? That doesn't make sense. A rich man or a beautiful woman can have anything or anyone they want."

"That's just the problem. When one has the power to get anything they want, they tend to set their goals on taking whatever they see that interests them. The things that can be 'seen' are the material things that only have passing value. These material things are supposed to bring the intangible goals of happiness, love, self fulfillment and peace; but the material things soon become the end instead of the means. As a result, the person continually reaches for satisfaction, only to find that each conquest is just another disappointment," the Priest philosophized.

"I'd like to see you try to convince a jury with that argument," scoffed the detective.

"I've been trying to convince people of this fact of life ever since I was ordained," Broadhurst came back. "Most accept the theory but only superficially. It has been said that one can not find happiness until they first experience sadness! It is a matter of appreciation. There is no easy road, and there are no short cuts. Perhaps if you are fortunate enough to suffer early in life, you may find peace and happiness as you grow older."

"If I was a rich man and had a beautiful wife, I wouldn't ask for anything more," retorted Morelli.

"I've heard those sentiments from many, many people; but never from a rich man or a beautiful woman!" countered Broadhurst.

AT THE POLICE STATION

Father Broadhurst entered Morelli's office slightly out of breath. "What's the big news you have for me?" he asked.

"I think I have solved the case! I've just arrested Samuel Johnson, Holly's last husband, for her murder." Morelli had a self-satisfied look on his face and anxiously waited for his friend to ask him to explain further.

"Are you sure?" questioned the cleric in a low, doubting tone. "I know Sam Johnson, and I can tell you that he is no murderer."

Morelli could hardly wait to explain his case. "The break came when Mag Horrihan tipped me off that Sam had been hounding Holly, trying to get her to come back with him. The night before the murder, Mag broke up a yelling match between them and as Sam left, he said—If I can't have you, no one else will have you either."

"And you have arrested Sam on that evidence?" Father Broadhurst bellowed in an uncharacteristically harsh tone.

"Certainly not," snapped Morelli. "We found the coil of nylon rope that matched the piece used to strangle Holly hidden in his home. Our Lab matched the piece used for the murder with the coil at Sam's house and there is absolutely no question, the murder weapon belongs to Sam Johnson!"

Father Broadhurst was noticeably shaken. He quickly left the detective's office without uttering another word and headed for the jail where Sam Johnson was being held.

AT THE JAIL HOUSE

Sam sat on his bunk with his hands on his head as Father Broadhurst arrived. When Sam looked up and saw the priest, he started to cry. "Honest, Father! I never touched Holly, and I never touched that rope. I never saw that rope before in my life."

"What is your connection with Mag Horrihan?" the Priest asked in a low, calm voice.

Sam looked down at the floor, obviously embarrassed. "She and I, that is, the both of us were in love with Holly. Every time Holly and I started to get to the point where we were going to get back together for good, Mag would come along and turn everything upside down."

Short Stories and Tall Tales 101

"Ummm," groaned the Priest in deep thought. "Basically the modern love triangle."

There was an awkward silence for a couple of minutes, then the Priest sat up straight. "Did you say that you never even touched that coil of rope?"

"Never!"

"I'll be back," Broadhurst said as he quickly left for Morelli's office.

BACK AT THE DETECTIVE'S OFFICE

Broadhurst busted into Morelli's Office. "Did you check the rope for fingerprints?"

Morelli was startled and didn't say a word.

"Did you check the rope for fingerprints?" Broadhurst demanded.

"Why no," stammered the bewildered Detective.

"They you had better do it right away!"

Morelli called in an assistant and ordered the finger printing to be done immediately.

After a wait that seemed like hours, the assistant returned. Well, what did you find?" the impatient Detective asked.

"There were two prints on the rope, both women's prints!" the assistant answered.

"Both women?" the Priest blurted out.

"Who?" demanded Morelli

"Holly Malloy and Mag Horrihan," said the assistant.

"Mag Horrihan!" the Detective and the Priest yelled simultaneously.

In less than an hour, Sam Johnson was released and Mag Horrihan was arrested for the murder of Holly Malloy.

AT THE RECTORY

Father Broadhurst opened the door and welcomed Detective Morelli into the Rectory. "What is the important development in the case that you wanted to tell me?" the anxious Priest asked.

"I've just released Mag Horrihan! She had a perfect alibi the entire weekend that Holly was killed. It seems that both she andSam had an ongoing relationship with Holly. Mag discovered the body and planted the coil of rope in Sam's house. She was sure that Sam did it and we are checking the evidence again to see if there are any other fingerprints."

"I'm sure you won't find Sam's prints," Broadhurst interrupted.

Just then the telephone rang. "It's for you," the Priest said.

It was a short message. As Morelli put down the phone he looked at Broadhurst with a sick grin; "They found another print– but it isn't Sam's. The print belongs to another woman and they are checking it out now.

"Another woman!" exclaimed the Priest.

"Yes, this case is getting more bizarre the further we go into it," the Detective moaned.

At the Police Station

Father Broadhurst waited for word from Morelli for what seemed like an unreasonable length of time, then decided to go down to the Detective's Office himself to see what was going on. As he entered the office, Morelli was lecturing a young secretary that worked in the Police Lab.

"This young lady broke all of the rules and handled evidence in the Lab without plastic gloves on. There is no way that she can be connected to this case, but she has violated police rules, and around here that's a crime."

"Call it what you will," Broadhurst interrupted, "But the real crime has been solved. Holly Malloy was a disillusioned young lady that took her own life, just as I told you in the beginning."

Morelli was embarrassed to think that the Priest was right and searched for a retaliation.

"And she was murdered because of love," he finally blurted out.

"That wasn't love," the Priest retorted; "That was obsession. Some experts call it 'possessive love,' but love has no part in it. They both wanted Holly for their own selfish desires. They didn't care about Holly's feelings, and Holly became their victim.

"I guess a Priest is always right," Morelli snapped with clenched jaw, "Case Closed!"

A CATASTROPHIC OBSESSION

****

The Army Hummer came to a screeching halt in front of the check point where Charlie and his buddy were stationed and the Sergeant shouted out,

"A car bomber just killed 100 soldiers at headquarters! Be on the alert! It looks like all hell is breaking loose!"

No cars came close to the two guardsmen that evening, but sometime later, a little old Iraqi woman, or what looked like a little old Iraqi woman, came up to the station to wish them well; and the two soldiers were blown to eternity. They said that it was quick and painless. It was quick, but it wasn't painless. Part of the pain traveled half way around the world to Charlie's wife, Christine, in a little town in upstate New York.

Charlie was in the National Guard several years ago before marrying Christine and celebrating the birth of Charlie Jr.

The baby was just four days old when Charlie got that fateful letter from the Commander in Chief that told him to report to his old unit for duty in Iraq.

Now it was just Christine with an infant son who had to pick up the pieces and carry on. There was no place for her to go except to move back in with her parents, something she swore she would never do when her father disowned her for marrying Charlie.

****

Chapter I

The first few weeks after the news of Charlie's horrible death, Christine was in shock. From all appearances, she was a very strong young lady who was taking all of this in stride. She was indeed strong and proud as she watched the President on TV reassuring all that these deaths would not be in vain, and that we will hold steadfast to our resolve to win the war no matter how long it takes; But Christine's appearance was only a front. As time wore on, she awakened to the reality of the situation and entered a phase of deep depression.

Christine's evening walk was the highlight of her day. Her heart sank as she passed the funeral home that had been closed by the new owner who had consolidated the business with his other establishment. Charlie had developed the "Home" into a most respectable business and they were so proud of his accomplishment. And there, behind the old factory was the Salvation Army Social Center. Charlie got his start at the Center after "graduating" from reform school.

On this evening, Christine just stood before the old building for several minutes thinking about Charlie and how much she missed him. As she was standing there, the Captain came by and greeted her.

"Why hello, Christine!" he said as he approached. "I am so sorry about Charlie. What a terrible, terrible tragedy!"

The sobbing girl just looked at the Captain without saying a word. It seemed that she just couldn't talk. The Captain sensed her plight and invited her into his office.

Once into the plain, but comfortable office, Christine regained her composure. "How could God allow such a thing like this to happen?" she blurted out.

The Captain had heard questions like this many, many times before. He found that the best response was to look compassionate and not utter a word. However, silence in this case didn't seem to work. Finnaly, after several ineffective moans to show extra concern, he decided to offer a bit of philosophy.

"God doesn't allow these things," he said, "It is man's misuse of Gods gifts that causes these tragedies."

This just didn't seem to satisfy Christine and she countered with, "What do you think about this war?"

It was against the Captain's policy to discuss politics but it would just be rude and insensitive not to respond.

"War is hell!" the Captain answered. "Jesus tells us to turn the other cheek and to love our enemies, but few men have the character and strength to follow his teaching."

"At least Charlie was killed by the enemy and it wasn't another accident," Christine nervously butted in.

The Captain was a bit puzzled by this response and quietly waited for Christine to continue.

"At least he was awarded the Purple Heart," she asserted. "That is an honor that no one can take away from him. It must be awful for those families whose husbands and sons were killed in accidents with nothing to show for their deaths."

It would have been so easy to just pass over this with reassuring words, but the officer felt that it might be a betrayal to those who were serving and whose deaths came indirectly rather than by specific enemy action.

"I have always had great respect for those who received the purple heart as I have for all of our armed forces who served in combat." The Captain, who had served in Vietnam before joining the Salvation Army, continued. "I have always felt sympathy for the Purple Heart people! We were all doing our duty, serving in harms way, and most of us were lucky and didn't have to receive a Purple Heart. Personally I felt that the best award of all was the GI Bill."

Christine had mixed emotions. Charlie was a hero! He gave his life! The suicide bomber was dressed like a woman and deceived Charlie and his partner. It didn't seem to her that the Captain had given all of the honor and respect that Charlie deserved! She shortly bid the Captain farewell and returned home.

The Captain felt that Christine was not pleased with his reaction to Charlie's award and it disturbed him greatly. He certainly respected Charlie; the way he had pulled himself up by the boot straps and answered the call of his Commander in Chief, even though he didn't believe that the action the Commander in Chief had taken was sufficient basis for complete honor and respect as far as he was concerned. The fact that Charlie was killed by a suicide bomber did not seem to be the major accomplishment of his life.

Short Stories and Tall Tales   109

When the Captain went home that evening, he discussed the Purple Heart issue with his wife Laura. After careful thought, Laura offered, "Perhaps I shouldn't say this, but I think that the Purple Heart Award is actually an attempt by the leadership in the society to divert attention away from the enormous sacrifice that they have demanded of its common place citizens."

The Captain was a bit taken back by this revelation. "Of course you have the right to express your opinion, that is what true Democracy and Freedom is all about. But, I believe that all citizens are required to make this sacrifice if needed," he countered..

"Not exactly," Laura continued; "All government officials plus those in the society that they feel are essential for the operation of society are exempt. This is what is called "Leadership from the Rear. Even you, yourself, are now exempt as a clergyman."

Somehow the Captain hadn't thought of himself as a clergyman although he received religious training to obtain his commission as a Salvation Army Officer, and part of his duties were to conduct religious services. He had been raised in a "high" Protestant Church with all of the pomp and ceremony that goes with this type of religion. He had left the Church when special interest groups joined the leadership and he felt that the Church had become more of a political organization hiding behind the "Cross" than a Christian society following the teachings of Christ. The "Army" with its commitment to feed and cloth the poor and meet the needs of others fulfilled his search for a purpose in life when he returned home from Vietnam..

"But how does all of this relate to the Purple Heart." he thought. Regardless of whether or not the Purple Heart was another method used by the Leadership to manipulate the masses, it was viewed by many as an almost sacred symbol of patriotism and courage; and it would be criminal to do anything to taint that image. He would see Christine again and somehow atone for any harm that he may have done.

CHAPTER II

Months went by and Christine's depression lingered on. She had been to a Psychiatrist, a Psychologist and a Spiritual Advisor, but nothing seemed to help.

"You need to forget about Charlie and get on with your life," her father advised. "Look around! You've got everything one could want for. A beautiful home, a beautiful son, and enough money to take care of all of your needs and wishes,-- and then some."

"Money isn't everything," Christine came back. "It's more than that!"

The old man was about ready to break out laughing but saw that his daughter was truly serious and held his emotions.

"Life should have a purpose!" she continued. "It's more than the selfish desire to fill all of our wishes with candy and toys. Charlie used to say that it was what we did for others that was what really counted."

Her father threw up his hands and walked away.

Christine mulled in her mind some of the serious conversations she and Charlie had had. She recalled that he felt he had found happiness when he did something that was helping others. His training to be a MET in Reform School was the real beginning of his life, he would say. And as a funeral director, he was able to bring comfort to those suffering the greatest grief in this life, the loss of a loved one. What she needed to do was to find a way to help those in need; but what could she do. She was a complete failure in the funeral business, and she had no training to do anything else. Perhaps there was something she could do to help the poor and unfortunate.

When the Captain received a call from Christine, he felt that it was the hand of God giving him the chance to atone for the hurt he had inflicted when talking with her about Charlie's Purple Heart.

"Tomorrow morning will be fine," he said. "I look forward to seeing you!"

When Christine arrived the next morning, she was awkwardly quiet. The Captain broke the ice with, "We have Charlie's picture with a picture of his Purple Heart hanging in our dining hall. Come, let me show you." They proceeded to the dining hall with the Captain keeping up a nervous chatter.

"Charlie was one of the most successful souls to pass through our hall. He gave generously to our support after he became a successful businessman. I thought a lot of Charlie and I respected him greatly." Christine was very pleased with the picture of Charlie and his purple

heart. She had a much warmer feeling toward the Captain now and felt more comfortable in discussing the reason for her visit.

"I've been quite depressed the last few months," she started. "I would like to have a purpose in my life, and, perhaps I could do something to help in the work here."

The Captain paused for a bit and seemed to be thinking of something that Christine could do. Actually, he was thinking, "I know that her intentions are good, but good intentions by themselves are not enough. There is more truth than poetry in the old saying, 'the road to hell is paved with good intentions.' Christine would most likely require more care to be given to her than she would give to others;

However, that is not exactly the point, Christine needs help and getting involved, and trying to meet the needs of others is the medicine that she needs right now."

"I'm sure that you would be a great help here," he finally responded. "What do you feel that you would like to do?"

Christine hadn't really thought much about anything specifically that she could do but she felt that she should make some sort of meaningful suggestion. "Perhaps I could counsel some of the young ladies," she stated in a questioning tone.

Out of every ten people who volunteer their services, the Captain found that half would look for something that would make them look good, and usually that they would like to do something in an advisory capacity. One of the times when a young man volunteered to actually work and to shovel off the walk after a snow storm, he literally jumped up from his chair with surprise. A good share of the time it is a case of helping the volunteer helper rather than the helping of those that they volunteer to help.

"We have a full staff of counselors." he answered trying to discourage her from that line of thought and yet not dampen her enthusiasm to help others.

"We have work around the office that we can always use help with; would you like to do that?"

Short Stories and Tall Tales   113

This wasn't exactly the kind of meaningful work that Christine had in mind and the Captain understood this immediately.

"We have to make up three hundred food baskets to distribute to needy families! It's hard work and not a very exciting job but it fills a great need," he quickly suggested.

"Three hundred families needing food baskets in our town!" she squeaked. There aren't even one hundred families on the whole south side!"

The "south side" was the recognized "poor section" of the town. The Captain showed no sign of surprise at her apparent unawareness of the situation in their town and calmly stated, "There are many people in need that are not at the bottom of the poverty level. Many of the working people who have lost good paying jobs and now have to settle for minimum wage are struggling to keep from loosing everything they have worked so hard for. They find that the assistance we and others like the City Mission give to them allow them to keep their heads above water. They make too much to apply for food stamps and other government help, but not enough to survive without loosing their homes and other possessions.

Suddenly a thought hit the Captain; "There is a lady from Rhowanda that will be working on the baskets also. She was a school teacher before she was forced to leave her country to survive but she was not fluent in English and had to take a lesser paying job in this country. She is very proud and will not accept charity. She insists on working whenever we give her food or clothing. I have been trying to help her with her English and perhaps you would like to work with her on this also!"

Christine was thrilled. This was the kind of help she would like to give, and it was the kind of activity that would help her with her depression.

Chapter III

The lady's name from Rhowanda was Josephine. She was a regal soul and she and Christine became fast friends. In a little less than a year, Christine was no longer depressed, and Josephine was ready to accept a job in the elementary school.

Christine's father did not appreciate Christine's relationship with Josephine and when Christine invited her to their Church he nearly blew a gasket. This did not phase Christine in the least, and the Sunday affair came and went without incident.

"Now you'll have to come with me next Sunday," Josephine said as the two parted.

"Where do you go to Church?" Christine asked, seemingly surprised that

Josephine had a Church.

"I've been going to the Army Citadel since shortly after moving here," she answered.

Christine pictured the social center services which were mostly attended by men, and some of them didn't seem like the people she wanted to attend Church with.

Josephine sensed Christine's apprehension and quickly added. "There's no incense or flowing robes, and some of the women wear funny bonnets, but the band and chorale group provide some beautiful music. I particularly like the "Testimony session" where individuals witness to a special blessing they have received that week."

Christine attended the service the following week with Josephine and was pleasantly surprised. However it wasn't exactly the kind of Church Service that she felt most comfortable with.

"I feel that "Communion is the main part of a church service and without it I don't feel that I have been to Church," Christine explained.

"I understand how you feel," Josephone responded. "I attended a church in my homeland before coming here and am aware of Christ's command at the last supper to 'do this in remembrance of me. But you know, there are several ways to observe this command. I have communion with every meal I eat! I pray before every meal thanking God for his blessings and remember the sacrifice of our Savior."

Christine was speechless. The two remained close friends, but on Sundays the two friends went their separate ways. Even best friends don't have to do everything together.

Over the next two months Christine made many friends including a close relationship with the Captain. She valued his counsel and felt that he was the major factor in her recovery from her deep depression. Now she was taking a much deeper look at the "Catastrophic Success" (the President's assessment of the War in Iraq.) She tried desperately to find a purpose for Charlie's sacrifice.

"It helped to keep us from being destroyed by an A Bomb," one of her friends told her. "We invaded Iraq to take away their weapons of Mass Destruction!"

No sooner had Christine began to appreciate Charlie's sacrifice to protect his country from weapons of mass destruction than the media exposed the fact that there were no weapons of mass destruction in Iraq and that none of the Terrorists that attacked us on 9/11 were from Iraq.

Christine went into another state of depression and renewed her quest to find a purpose for Charlie's sacrifice.

"We're helping the people of Iraq to gain Freedom and Democracy." was the next purpose to consider. Iraq finally did have a democratic election of sorts although it was a long way from establishing a democratic society. Democracy also seemed to be talked about in a couple of other Middle East countries. "But why did we have to kill so many people and destroy so much of the country; and why did we have to sacrifice so many of our troops to bring Peace and Democracy to a country half way around the world from us when most of their people didn't want democracy. Charlie was a funeral director, and an upstanding member of our society. Why was he forced to sacrifice his life to bring freedom and democracy to Iraq?'

"Democracy and Freedom is the answer to bring peace and save the world," was the battle cry from a radical religious group in the country. "The war in Iraq was fulfillment of God's will," this group concluded.

"Now it was God's will that Charlie was taken from Her?" Christine had just about reached the end of her rope and desperately sought guidance from the Captain.

Short Stories and Tall Tales 117

The Captain tried to console his devastated friend but try as he would, he was not successful. Finally after deep concern and consideration he quietly suggested, "Perhaps you should discuss your thoughts with Bill. I am an advocate of the separation of Church and State and try to stay out of politics."

"Bill!" Christine screeched as she usually did to express her belief that what she heard was preposterous

Bill was an elderly man who drove one of the trucks that pick up goods that are donated to the "Army" to sell at their Thrift Store. He was clean and gentlemanly but she hardly thought of him as an intellectual with anything to contribute to a discussion at this level.

"Bill is one of the most brilliant men I have ever met," the Captain countered. "He was a child genius and became a college professor at a very young age. He then left college to go into business and became a millionaire. A few years ago after three unsuccessful marriages, he was 'born again,' and took a somewhat more difficult path than most born again people take. He anonymously gave nearly all of his possessions to the poor and after a short time spent "on the street' mingling with the 'fallen' in our society, he joined with us and volunteered to give his life to God. He has a Bible verse on the wall over his bed that says, 'In as much as ye have done it to the least of these thy brethren, you have done it unto me.'

He is as completely devoted to the will of God as any person I have ever heard of, and he has a clear picture of God's Will."

Christine did become acquainted with Bill and they did indeed have a number of deep discussions. She became much wiser and intently studied Charlie's catastrophic death.

" We have to respect the rights of others even when it seems that they are just not doing things right," Bill convinced her.

"No one has the right to impose their will on others no matter how noble and self righteous they feel they are. Even God doesn't force his will on man.

"Bill did not want to tell Christine how to judge society, he chose to ask her questions and let her make up her own mind. "Everything depends upon your perspective, the way you look at it," he told her.

"There's at least two sides to every issue. It takes great wisdom to look beyond the two devils, deceit and deception, to see things clearly; to understand the true meaning of a situation."

"Is a man who is forced to sacrifice his life in battle by the Commander in Chief of a Democracy any more free than a man who is forced to sacrifice his life in battle by a Dictator?

Who is the greatest hero, a man who steps on a land mine or one who has an accident while driving through hostile territory to bring needed supplies to the troops?

It is amazing how narrow minded one can become when they don't stop to think things out for themselves; and it is amazing how indifferent one can be when rationalizing for their own personal welfare and their own personal preferences.

Christine did not follow Bill's logic. As far as she could see, there was only one side to all of these questions and Bill sensed this.

"Christine," he reasoned, "Let me tell you a little story to better explain what I am trying to say. This story is about two Irishmen, named Pat and Mike."

"Oh no, not another Irish joke," Christine thought to herself.

Bill continued. "These men worked for the Department of Public Works and on this particular day they were digging a ditch in front of the local house of 'Ill Repute.' As they were digging, the local Rabbi came walking up the street. Both men watched as the Rabbi went into the house of ill repute. Pat turned to Mike and said, 'Ain't it a shame, but what can you expect from those heathen.'

A little while later the Reverend Foster D. Perkins came walking up the street and both men watched as the Reverend Perkins went into the house of ill repute.Again Pat turned to Mike and said, 'Ain't it a shame, but what can you expect from those heathen.'

Some time later, the good Father Patrick J. O'Sullivan came walking up the street. "I'm not going to look," said Pat; "Neither am I," said Mike. Then, both men looked up over the top of the hole, and faith and begorra, the good Father Patrick J. O'Sullivan went into the house of ill repute.

There was a long silence in that hole and two very long Irish faces. Finally, Pat turned to Mike and said. "Ain't it a shame, one of those poor little prostitutes must be seriously ill!"

Christine laughed, and she understood Bill's point. Everything does depend upon the way you look at it. We can be biased and even bigoted with hardly realizing it unless we look at things with an open mind. Bill went on, "The good intentions of man will not save the world, it has been wisely said that the road to hell is paved with good intentions. Judas, himself, no doubt had good intentions when he betrayed Christ in the Garden of Gethsemine. Many Biblical scholars have theorized that Judas wanted Christ to use his great power to conquer the world. The message here is that we cannot impose our will on God, we must impose God's will in our own lives. The divinity of Christ was clearly revealed shortly before the betrayal when Jesus prayed and asked that he be excused from his given task, but he concluded with, 'not my will but thy will be done.' God's will is in his Word.

"How do we know that waging the war in Iraq to bring democracy and freedom like we have to those people wasn't Gods will?" Christine asked. "How do we know what God's will is?

Bill rubbed his chin and paused for a moment. "First of all, we do not have a Democracy, we have a Republic."

Christine looked at Bill as if he had lost his marbles. "Isn't a Republic a Democracy?"

"Not at all," Bill countered. "In a Republic, the government officials are elected by the people, but then the officials rule with near absolute power during their term of office if the Congress doesn't intervene. Actually, we do not even have a true Republic. We have an electoral college system that can, and has over-ridden the democratic election by the people. Our President who declared war on Iraq did not receive the majority vote of the people, the basic principle of a democracy.

Christine was flabergasted! "But what of God's Will?"

"If you are thinking in terms of Christianity," Bill replied, "Christ did not condone war and violence. In fact, even the other religion that we are fighting against does not advocate violence. Both Christ and Mohammed taught love and peace!"

Again Christine was truly shaken. "What about the Church leaders and government leaders on both sides who claim to be doing God's Will?" she asked.

Bill answered, "They are other extremists following their own will. Both suicide and preemptive strike are a violation in both religions."

Christine was noticeably angry and distraught. "How could our government make such a terrible mistake and cause the sacrifice of so many innocent lives?

Bill paused for a moment, then responded. "An obsession is a powerful drive that clouds good judgment; and fundamental truths; and values are often completely ignored as well. When a person entrusted with the lives of others carries their obsession to the extreme, and forces others into harms way, it can become a "catastrophic obsession."

Christine was beginning to understand more about Charlie's sacrifice and it gave her closure, but it did not give her peace. Perhaps closure is about all that she could expect in this case.

Printed in the United States
48111LVS00006B/31-36